Rayne's Redemption

By Linda Shenton Matchett

Chapter One

Drenched to the skin, Rayne Dalton stood in the pouring rain and wrapped her arms around her middle as her twin sister was lifted into the ambulance. Concern etched on the physician's forehead belied his earlier words of comfort during his examination of Jessica as she lay unconscious on the cannery floor. He'd given up his attempts to get Rayne to return to her workstation. It had only been her and Jessica since their parents died in the awful Independence Day fire five years ago. She had no plans to leave her sister alone, waking up in a hospital room filled with strangers.

Rayne approached the open-walled carriage and hiked up her skirts with her left hand while she grabbed the side of the conveyance with her right. She climbed onto the step and hefted herself inside.

Dr. Uxley's head jerked up. "What do you think you're doing?"

"You get out of that ambulance, Miss Dalton," Mr. Cross, the manager of her section in the cannery, bellowed from the curb. "It's bad enough you've wasted time watching the docs work on that sister of yours. I'm not paying you to play nurse."

Ignoring the doctor for the moment, she glared at the diminutive man whose close-set eyes and twitching nose were reminiscent of the mice that haunted the corners of the damp, dark building that held her and Jessica captive for twelve hours a day, six days a week. "I'm not playing nurse. I'm accompanying my sister to the hospital to ensure she receives the care she needs. I'll return to work tomorrow."

"Miss—"

She whirled and held up her hand to the doctor. "Don't tell me I can't come with you. The longer we dawdle, the less chance my sister has. Wouldn't you agree, Doctor?"

He pressed his lips together and shrugged, apparently loathe to give her a straight answer about her sister's condition.

Turning back to Mr. Cross, she pointed her finger at the man. "I wouldn't have to leave work if you and the rest of those money-hungry men who run this cannery didn't cut corners with regard to safety. Jessica wouldn't have been injured if the machinery was regularly maintained. It's your fault she's hurt."

The man's face darkened, and he suddenly seemed to notice the growing crowd on the sidewalk. "How dare you make those baseless accusations. Your sister's carelessness is the reason she's lying in that ambulance. Now, get back to work immediately or you're fired."

Rayne's stomach hollowed. Living without Jessica's salary would be difficult, but if neither of them were making an income, they'd be out on the streets in a matter of weeks. Her gaze tripped from her employer to her sister's ashen face. No. She wouldn't abandon the only person she had left in the world.

"Then I guess I'm fired, Mr. Cross. Family comes first." She plunked down on the bench next to the doctor and crossed her arms.

"You'll regret this, Miss Dalton." A triumphant gleam sparked in the manager's eyes. "When you're down to your last nickel, don't come crying to me for a job."

"And risk my life, too? No, thank you." She'd figure out something. She always did. Whereas Jessica was the sweet, pliable one of the two of them, Rayne was the fighter, the one who ensured they had enough to eat and a roof over their heads. Scrimping what little money they received as assembly-line workers at the cannery, she often bartered to provide for them. Running errands, doing chores, taking in laundry, and any other job she could find.

Straightening, the doctor patted Rayne's shoulder, then banged on the cab of the vehicle. "Let's go."

The ambulance lurched forward, and Jessica moaned. Her eyelids fluttered but remained closed. Dr. Uxley leaned over her and pressed his stethoscope against her chest.

Rayne blinked back tears. Crying wouldn't do anyone any good. Least of all her sister. She fisted her hands and stifled the urge to push the doctor aside so she could envelope her sister in a hug, the two of them against the rest of humanity, like always.

Several minutes later, the ambulance stopped in front of the four-story hospital. An Italian Gothic structure with imposing towers made of brick and granite, the mammoth building was the largest at the west end of Portland. White-clad figures rushed in and out of the double-door entrance, two of whom trotted toward the ambulance.

Dr. Uxley jumped to the ground, then turned and assisted Rayne from the vehicle. The pair of orderlies, beefy men with bearlike hands, climbed inside, hoisted the stretcher from the bench, and exited with more speed and grace than she expected. She followed the trio into the building.

"Rayne?" Her sister's voice was low and raspy.

"I'm here, Jessica." She pushed past the doctor and came alongside the stretcher. "I won't leave you."

Jessica's wan face relaxed, and she sighed.

"Miss Dalton, you must allow us space to tend to your sister." The doctor gestured to a door, and Rayne stepped aside to let the men enter the room. He paused on the threshold. "Give me ten minutes."

"Please let her stay."

Rayne's head whipped toward the gurney where Jessica's litter now rested. "You heard her, Doctor; I'm not going anywhere. However, I'll stand in the corner."

Dr. Uxley's lips thinned, and he nodded. "Fine, but only as a means to keep your sister calm." He turned on his heel and walked into the room. A nurse stood near a counter holding a glass bottle. He held his hands over a basin, and the woman poured a clear liquid over his skin. He shook fingers to shed excess moisture, then hurried to Jessica's side.

Minutes crawled past as the man bent over her sister, his tall form blocking his ministrations from Rayne. Her stomach roiled, and she wrapped her arms around her belly. What was taking so long? He'd stemmed the bleeding at the cannery. How much more care did Jessica need? Did she dare say a prayer to her sister's God? Would He hear her and intervene for one of His children or would He ignore Rayne's plea?

Chapter Two

"Hand me those lanterns, Alonzo." Flynn Wade stood midway up the ladder in the storage room of the mercantile. If he didn't keep busy, he'd jump out of his skin, so he attacked the project he'd been putting off for months: organizing his inventory, a tedious but necessary task if he was to keep track of which merchandise hadn't flown off the shelves.

"These?" His best friend, Alonzo Lawton, held up a pair of brass lamps that had appeared prettier in the catalog, evidenced by the fact no one had purchased them since they'd arrived three months ago.

Flynn blew out a sigh and reached for the offending items. "Yes. Let's give the customers a break from looking at them until I figure out how to make them more attractive."

"Slashing the price would be a start." Alonzo grinned. "Or maybe paying a customer to take them off your hands."

"Clever." Hands on his hips, Flynn surveyed the room. A conglomeration of canned goods, household items, and tools crowded every inch of the shelves. His clients appreciated the fact he carried much of what they needed rather than requiring them to make an order and wait for their purchases.

In the beginning, cash flow had been tight while the folks of Rocky Mountain Springs decided whether or not they could trust the young Englishman who'd given up his homestead claim to set up shop in their town. He'd discovered after his first growing season that he had a better head for finances than for farming, so when Alonzo had indicated a desire to expand his property, Flynn had sold to the young man without a second thought.

One by one people in town came into the store to snoop, eventually making purchases. Word filtered through the community that his pricing was fair and he had a large selection. Their suspicions had cooled, and he now counted many of his customers as friends.

The clock chimed, muffled behind the curtain that separated the storage room from the mercantile, and Flynn's gaze shot to the doorway. His heart pounded. The train bearing his future bride would be arriving in less than an hour.

"You look like a man headed for his execution." Alonzo chuckled. "Shouldn't you be jumping for joy?"

With a shrug, Flynn shoved the lanterns onto the shelf, then climbed down the ladder. He leaned against the wall and crossed his arms. "What if she takes one look at me and gets back on the train?"

Alonzo cocked his head and rubbed his jaw in mock rumination. "You're handsome enough. Not as good looking as me, of course, but she won't go running. I think you're safe."

"But I'm only a second son and a shopkeeper."

"Stop being so English. You're in the American West now. We don't care one whit about lineage and class. Well, some folks do, but most of us don't give two hoots about those things. Besides, you told her about yourself in the letters, and she's accepted your proposal. She wouldn't have come if she didn't want to spend the rest of her life with you."

"Or I'm an avenue out of the cannery. Her descriptions about the place are frightening. A dark, dangerous job. Her twin sister works there, too." Flynn raked his fingers through his hair. "Perhaps the chance to live in the open spaces of Wyoming is more appealing than hunkering over a piece of equipment for years on end. I'm glad to rescue her, but is that all our marriage will be?"

"You're borrowing trouble. All you've talked about for weeks is your bride. How much you have in common, and not just your faith in God. Suddenly you have cold feet."

"Weren't you nervous the day Rhea arrived?"

"No, we were in love, and I knew she was the girl for me."

Flynn narrowed his eyes. "Not just a little? You'd never met."

"Okay, so maybe I was a tad skittish, but we'd exchanged letters for months, and I knew our marriage would work out."

"That's the difference. Jessica and I have only written four letters. Not enough to develop feelings for one another."

"Which is why you agreed to take your time to court and not marry right away. If this is the woman God has for you, everything will work out."

"And if she's not?"

"We'll cross that prairie when we need to." Alonzo gestured to the door. "Now, go get washed up so we can meet the train."

The tightness in Flynn's chest eased, and he nodded. Slipping through the cloth doorway, he entered the store, then stopped. Bright and roomy, the mercantile was neat and clean, the wooden floor free of dirt, and the shelves and products free of dust. A rainbow of fabric bolts were piled on the far table, and cans of every shape, size, and color lined the shelves and counters. Bags of feed were stacked by the door, ensuring customers didn't have to carry them a long distance to their wagons.

A pair of elderly women stepped inside, the bell jangling as the door opened. "Good afternoon, Mr. Wade." The taller of the two waved a scrap of paper. "We're here to obtain supplies for next month's quilting bee."

The distant shriek of the train whistle split the air. Flynn glanced at the clock. Early, of all days. Should he leave Alonzo to fumble his way through the order? No, that could produce disastrous results. But sending his friend to meet his bride was no solution either. Was it?

"Flynn." Alonzo's voice held a note of warning.

"I've got a business to run. Surely, she'll understand that." Flynn gestured to the quilters. "I won't be long. You meet Miss Dalton and bring her back to the store. I'll be done by the time you return."

"All right, but don't say I didn't caution you." Alonzo grabbed his hat from the hook by the door and headed into the dusty street.

"Okay, ladies. Let's see that list. I'm sure we can find you some lovely fabrics." Minutes passed as he selected material from the table, cut the desired yardage, then put aside the bolt. The bell tinkled again, and he glanced toward the sound. A young woman dressed in a silk dress and hat hesitated in the doorway, a tentative expression on her face. "I'll be with you in a moment."

"Thank you. I'm looking for Mr. Wade."

He gaped the woman, her English accent triggering memories of London. "I'm Flynn Wade, and you're a long way from home."

"I'm Blythe St. George. Your parents sent me. Didn't you get their letter? They arranged for me to come to America to marry you."

Chapter Three

Rayne licked her dry lips as Mr. Lawton held open the mercantile door. If her prospective groom was as nice as the polite man he'd sent to retrieve her, she had nothing to worry about. Her companion smiled and motioned for her to enter. She stepped into the store and almost bumped into a regal-looking woman wearing a gorgeous red dress and a fashionable hat that sat at a jaunty angle on her intricately styled hair. So much for the assumption that everyone in the West wore homespun and bonnets.

Aware of her own travel-weary appearance, Rayne smoothed her skirts as she surveyed the store seeking the man who expected her sister. Behind a table stacked with fabric, a towering, bearded man gaped at the woman in front of her. His gaze flicked to Rayne, then back to the woman. The tension in the room was as thick as fleas on a dog's back.

Was the man at the counter Mr. Wade? He appeared to work in the shop and was the only male visible. Hesitant to interrupt, she clutched her reticule and glanced at Mr. Lawton who seemed equally uncertain.

"What did you say?" The bearded man laid down his scissors and approached the woman in red, a frown creasing his forehead.

"Your parents sent me, Mr. Wade. They've reached an agreement for us to marry."

Rayne gasped, then slapped her hand over her mouth. This handsome man with the raven-black hair was her husband-to-be, yet the chic woman claimed she was betrothed to him. What was going on? Nausea threatened, and she swallowed to prevent her lunch reappearing. Had Mrs. Crenshaw made a mistake?

"I'm sorry you've traveled all this way for nothing, Miss St. George, but I'm committed to someone. In fact, she's arriving on the train that—" Mr. Wade's eyes widened, and his head swiveled toward Mr. Lawton, then Rayne. He stiffened and seemed to grow taller. "You...you're Miss Dalton. You're from the agency."

Emotions warred on Mr. Wade's face. Why did he seem surprised to see her? He'd sent his friend retrieve her.

Across the room, two gray-haired women watched the proceedings, and Rayne cringed. How soon before the biddies broadcast the drama to eager ears in town? She leaned toward Mr. Lawton and whispered, "Can we hold this conversation elsewhere?"

"Oh, my. I forgot about the Delaney sisters. Just a moment." He rushed to the two women and murmured something. They looked disappointed but nodded and made their way through the aisles, then out of the shop while Mr. Wade continued to stare goggle-eyed at her and the other woman. Mr. Lawton flipped the CLOSED sign, then locked the door. "Flynn, may I introduce Miss Jessica Dalton. Miss Dalton, this is Mr. Flynn Wade." He glanced at the woman in red. "I beg your pardon, but you have me at a loss."

Rayne swallowed. Would she ever get used to her new identify?

Her face mottled, the woman's expression was pinched. "Miss Blythe St. George, from England."

"Miss St. George. Lovely to meet you. May I assume you also came in on the one o'clock train?"

"Yes. I arranged for my bags to be taken to the Crescent Hotel, but it appears I won't be staying after all."

Mr. Wade finally seemed to gain his bearings as he blinked and gestured for everyone to take a seat near the woodstove in the middle of the room. Larger than any she'd ever seen, the iron behemoth sat cold and silent on the temperate May afternoon.

Rayne hesitated, her pulse racing. How could this have happened? Did Mr. Wade really know nothing about the arrangement with Miss St. George? What kind of parents didn't inform their son they'd selected a bride for him? She gulped. Coming from England, perhaps the woman was the better choice, and Rayne should take the next train out of town. But to where?

Jessica claimed that God was in control, yet on the very same train Rayne had taken to meet her intended, a woman from the man's homeland arrived to stake a claim. Perhaps God was not as powerful as her sister thought. Hot tears pricked the backs of her eyes. With her dying breath, Jessica insisted Rayne come to Wyoming in her place, asserting that this was an answer to her prayer. Whatever *this* was, it couldn't possibly be the result of a plea to the Almighty.

"Miss Dalton, please join us." Flynn motioned to the young woman clutching her reticule and looking like she might dash out the door. "I'm sure the situation is highly upsetting for you, and it is not how I planned for us to meet, but please come sit down."

"All right." She drew herself to her full height and walked with panther-like grace to the wooden chairs grouped near the Franklin stove. Tall and statuesque, the brown-haired beauty with the golden-brown eyes and porcelain skin rivaled any of the girls from England's drawing rooms, including Miss St. George. Her skirts rustled as she walked, and he caught the crisp scent of her soap as she slipped past him.

Flynn waited until she was seated before he lowered himself onto the last vacant chair. He cleared his throat and turned toward Miss St. George. "Again, I must apologize for your arduous yet wasted journey to

America. I will pay for your hotel stay until you can make arrangements for your return trip. I cannot marry you no matter what sort of agreement my parents made with yours. They have no control over my life, and therefore the arrangement is invalid."

Prim and proper, Miss St. George dipped her head, the feathers on her hat waving like a sheaf of wheat. "I understand, and I'm sorry to have caused you any embarrassment."

"You didn't. If I wasn't already betrothed, I'd be honored to marry you." He sent her what he hoped was a reassuring smile. "You seem like a lovely, intelligent woman. Any man would want you."

Her cheeks pinked, and she shrugged.

He jerked his head toward Alonzo. "Perhaps Mr. Lawton could escort you to the station to purchase your return ticket and then take you to the hotel."

"If you don't mind, I'd rather not make any sudden decisions. Your parents have already wired funds to the establishment for my stay, and I'd like to consider my options. Frankly, I'm not anxious for another month-long ocean voyage so soon on the heels of my arrival."

"Oh, I...uh...understand. Well, at least let Alonzo get you settled, then perhaps we could have dinner or—"

She rose and drew her skirts around her. "There's no need to feel you have to entertain me while I'm here. Your responsibilities lie with Miss Dalton." She turned to his fiancée. "I wish you much happiness."

Chin held high, she glided to the door. Alonzo scrambled to his feet and with a wide-eyed glance at Flynn followed her outside.

An awkward silence blanketed the room, and Flynn rubbed the back of his neck. He swallowed a sigh and gave Miss Dalton a wry smile. "Is there any way we can pretend the incident with Miss St. George never happened?"

She sagged against the chair, relief evident on her face. "Probably not, but we can make an effort. I feel as if I've come at an inopportune time. If you'd like to start over, I can go to the hotel for the remainder of the day and come back tomorrow."

His face fell. Had the debacle with Miss St. George caused Miss Dalton to change her mind about coming to Wyoming? Would she flee on tomorrow's train? "I'd like to spend time with you, but you must be exhausted from your trip." He cocked his head and studied her. Even in a plain cotton dress with lines of fatigue on her face, she was gorgeous. "Would you mind staying for a little while to talk about the situation? Then I could get you settled at the hotel...uh...a different hotel."

"That would be fine." She drew her bag close to her stomach, her knuckles white.

"Thank you." The tightness in his chest eased, and he leaned forward. "I am glad you're here, despite the inauspicious beginning. As we discussed in our letters, we'll take some time to get acquainted. Some couples wed immediately, but I...uh...wanted you to have the opportunity to make a fully informed decision after experiencing what your life would be like if you stayed."

"That sounds reasonable." Her fingers continued to grip her reticule. "And you can ascertain if I would make an acceptable partner...er...wife." Her gaze swept the mercantile. "Your shop is much larger than I expected. Bright and airy. Many selections for the customers. They must appreciate the array of choices."

He surveyed the shelves with new eyes and smiled. She appeared to be pleased rather than disappointed. Dare he hope that she would grow to love the shop as much as he did? "The building was tiny at first, but as I gained more business, I was able to expand. However, I'm not creative with my displays and would appreciate your assistance with that. As a...uh...woman, you know what women like, what attracts them toward a product."

"You'd like me to work in the store?" Her brow wrinkled. "I thought I would manage the household."

"Not until after we're married. You'll stay at the hotel until then." He frowned. "Did you change your mind about helping me run the shop?"

"Change my mind?" Her eyes widened, and she paled further. "No, not at all. I forgot we talked about that. The long journey must have made me addle-brained. I'm sorry."

"No need to apologize. I'm rushing you. It is me who should beg your pardon." He fisted his hands in his lap. "I'd like us to be open and honest with each other. If something bothers you or isn't to your liking, I hope you'll tell me. If you decide you don't enjoy being part of the store, you must let me know. We have a mutual faith in God, but a successful marriage also depends on candidness. At least, that's what Alonzo tells me." He shrugged. "Anyway, I don't want to set a date for the wedding until I've had a chance to court you properly. Is that all right with you?" He might regret giving her time to change her mind, but he'd rather be alone than wed a woman who didn't want to be his wife.

Chapter Four

A light breeze thick with odors of damp soil, horses, leather, and something she couldn't identify tugged at Rayne's cloak, and she pulled the wrap closer. She passed a restaurant, and the more pleasant scent of dinner preparations wafted from the open window. She peeked inside at the small establishment that had cloth-covered tables topped with candles and gleaming dinnerware. Her eyes widened. Not luxurious but less primitive than she'd expected. Another assumption shattered.

Her head throbbed. Perhaps she should have tried harder to take a nap at the hotel, but after tossing and turning for nearly thirty minutes, she'd risen, grabbed her sketchbook, and escaped to the streets of the small town. Charcoal was her favorite medium, its stark black lines capturing the essence of a scene without the interference of color. She'd already drafted the gazebo, livery, and one side of Main Street. Drawing helped her process the world around her as well as push aside that with which she didn't want to deal. Namely, a certain Englishwoman who arrived as a gift to Mr. Wade.

Did he mean what he'd said? That he had no interest in the woman and planned to court Rayne. Her stomach hollowed. He didn't want her. He wanted Jessica. Could she be her sister? Surely, he had more in common with Miss St. George, someone from his own country who understood his background. And far more attractive and classy than Rayne could ever hope to be.

He'd said he was a second son. What did that mean? Did he think he had less value than his older brother? Was that why he'd crossed an ocean to set up a new life in America? She could relate to the desire for a fresh start, but why did he need one? Did he also have secrets?

She heaved a sigh, and her grip tightened on her pad. Too many questions. How could she unearth the answers? Did she want to?

The sun dipped toward the horizon, and she squinted against the glare. Turning on her heel, she hurried down the sidewalk toward the hotel, her feet clattering against the wood. The hours had gotten away from her, but with any luck she'd have time to wash off the afternoon's dust and perspiration.

Rayne pushed through the heavy mahogany door with the stained-glass window and entered the lobby. Her gaze ricocheted around the room, and she blew out a sigh of relief. Mr. Wade wasn't here. She hastened to her room and tossed the sketchbook on the bed, then stripped to her clothes to take a sponge bath. She rushed through her ablutions and glanced in the mirror for a final inspection of her appearance, reminded again of her too-tall height and nondescript brown hair and eyes. Her porcelainlike complexion was her one redeeming quality and hadn't faded despite hours trapped in the cannery.

The emerald-green dress was the best she owned, yet the garment didn't hold a candle to Miss St. George's attire. "Stop it, Rayne. You have him for an entire evening. Alone. You can make him like you."

She pinched her cheeks to give them some color, then whirled and snatched her reticule from the chair before leaving the room. Pressing a hand against her chest, she took a deep breath to calm her racing pulse. She descended into the lobby, a smile pinned to her lips. Her gaze darted around the cozy room, but her dinner companion was nowhere to be seen. She glanced at the ornate clock on the fireplace mantel. Three minutes past their appointed meeting time.

Couples strolled through the door to the restaurant while others sat in the upholstered furniture chatting and laughing. She spied a chair in the corner and sank into it. The cushions enveloped her, and she resisted the urge to recline.

Minutes crawled past. Five minutes. Then ten. Then fifteen. Her mouth dried. Had Mr. Wade changed his mind about her? Was he at the other hotel with Miss St. George? The least he could do was reject her in person.

The door opened with a bang, and her intended burst into the lobby. He yanked off his hat and surveyed the room, eyes wide. His string tie was askew, and his hair looked as if it had been combed with an egg beater. His gaze met hers, and he trotted across the room, dodging guests. "I'm sorry. I'm so sorry." He bowed and offered his arm. "Thank you for waiting."

Rayne pushed to her feet and tucked her hand in the crook of his elbow, his scent a mixture of leather, bay rum, and perspiration. "I was close to giving up."

He blushed to the roots of his hair and patted her hand. "I don't blame you. Tardiness is not usually one of my many faults." He led her into the dining room, and a young woman met them in the doorway.

She looked him up and down, a coy smile on her face. "Mr. Wade, how nice of you to join us this evening."

"Thank you. There will be two of us dining tonight."

The hostess's glance slid to Rayne, and her smile became forced. "Follow me." She took them to a small table near the window and handed them menus. "Tara will be with you shortly." With another smile at Mr. Wade, she flounced back to the door, her hips swaying like an oversized bell.

Shaking her head, Rayne studied the list of food choices. Would she have to worry about every woman in town flirting with her bridegroom? Why use an agency when there seemed to be no shortage of interested parties?

A waitress came and took their orders, and in a short time returned with two fragrant plates of steak, mashed potatoes, and string beans. A thick gravy spilled from the potatoes onto the rest of the food.

Salivating, Rayne picked up her fork as her stomach rumbled.

"Would you mind if I said grace?" Mr. Wade's eyebrow lifted.

"Of course." Her face flamed. "I don't know what came over me."

"If you're like me, you're ravenous, and the meal smells delicious." He grinned. "I promise it will be a short prayer."

She giggled and laid down her utensil, then tucked her hands in her lap and bowed her head like Jessica used to do. Jessica. Rayne's heart clenched, and her eyes welled. She blinked away the moisture.

"Father, thank You for bringing Miss Dalton here safely." Mr. Wade's voice was warm and friendly as if he were talking to someone seated at the table. "Thank You for the food that we're about to eat, and bless the hands that prepared it. Please guide us as we seek Your will. In the name of Your Son, amen."

Rayne raised her head. She couldn't afford another gaff like forgetting about grace. Jessica prayed all the time. Was Mr. Wade the same way? She scooped some of the potatoes into her mouth and moaned. Fluffy and flavorful, the concoction melted on her tongue.

"Pretty good, isn't it?" Mr. Wade began to eat. "Bet you thought this place wouldn't rival your Portland restaurants."

"I admit my expectations weren't high, but this is wonderful."

"René, the chef, is a Frenchman. Another one of us who came for the land, but discovered he isn't a farmer. But what he can do with food is a miracle." He wiped his mouth and took a sip of coffee. "Listen, I don't want the dinner to be all business, but I thought we could discuss the logistics of our...uh...courting."

"Are you this analytical about everything?" She cocked her head. "Did you want to draw up a contract?"

"What? No. Well, not unless you want to." His cheeks pinked again. "In your last letter, you talked about how difficult it was at the cannery with management constantly changing their decisions. I thought perhaps you might feel more at ease if we discussed expectations up front."

"How considerate. Thank you." Rayne picked up her glass with trembling hands. Would she be able to find the letters her sister had written? Did he keep them at the mercantile or at home? Knowing what Jessica said would help. "Whatever you think is best."

"I'd appreciate it if you could work at the mercantile until one o'clock each day. Mornings are our busiest times. Then you could have the afternoons to do as you wish. As you know, I teach the boys' Sunday school class before worship, and choir rehearsal is on Wednesdays following midweek prayer meeting. You'd expressed an interest in helping me with the boys, but we never discussed whether you like to sing."

She nearly choked on the water she'd been sipping. How could she teach stories she didn't know? She set down the glass and wiped her mouth. "I'm afraid I'm not much of a singer. In fact, I can't carry a tune at all." She shrugged. "But I could help with the children. I'd rather you did the teaching, being a man, but I could help them do crafts or keep them from getting too wiggly."

"Perfect." He grinned. "The boys are going to love you."

"If you say so." Rayne speared some green beans and poked them into her mouth. She knew nothing about the Bible and even less about wrangling children. How soon before he discovered her subterfuge?

Chapter Five

Flynn finished scraping the stubble off his neck, then wiped the blade with the towel laying on the dresser. He picked up the scissors and trimmed his beard, angling his face close to the mirror. Most men in town who sported facial hair let the bristles grow long and bushy, but he preferred a more groomed appearance. Was he being too fastidious or clinging to his European roots?

He shrugged and rubbed his face with a second towel, then tossed the two cloths in the overflowing basket he used for collecting dirty clothes. He grabbed his shirt from the bed and slipped into it, noting the frayed cuffs. The last of his clean shirts, the garment would have to do. He'd been so intent upon the preparations for Miss Dalton's...Jessica's...arrival, he'd forgotten to take his items to the laundress.

The hours they'd spent during dinner had flown past, seeming to be over in the blink of an eye. Despite spending days on the train, she'd been bright and clever, albeit more candid and, dare he say it, forceful than she'd been in her letters. Granted, their correspondence had been minimal, only four letters between them, but she hadn't spoken with the flowery expressiveness she used in the missives. Perhaps she was more fatigued than she let on. Should he have given her a night's rest before asking her to dine?

With the unexpected arrival of Miss St. George, he couldn't risk leaving Miss Dalton to her own devices last evening, to worry and wonder about the woman who claimed to be his bride. A woman who didn't seem in a hurry to leave Rocky Mountain Springs. Was her presence going to cause problems? His parents had outdone themselves with interfering this time.

Taking a brush to his hair, he tamed his unruly locks, then tucked his shirt into his pants and poked his feet into his boots. He needed to get Miss St. George out of town, if not on a ship, at least in a carriage. He blew out a breath and pointed to himself in the mirror. "You have got to get a handle on this situation. Courting Miss Dalton...Jessica...will provide more than enough challenge without the added complications of Mum's and Father's *gift*."

Jessica. The name rolled off his tongue. A lovely name for a beautiful woman. They hadn't exchanged photos while writing, agreeing that appearances didn't matter, but after the shock of seeing her in the mercantile had worn off, he'd been delighted at how pretty she was.

He frowned. However, did her perfection come with hearing loss? Crass as it was, he'd called out to her as she ascended to her room because he'd forgotten to tell her he'd escort her to the shop for her first morning. She'd turned to him only after he waved his arm. Would she be offended if he asked her? Wouldn't she have mentioned the ailment in her letters?

"Get going, Flynn. You've wasted enough time arguing with yourself, and if you're late a second time, Miss Dalton might not be as forgiving."

After one last glance at his reflection, he strode from the room, grabbed his Stetson off the hook by the door, and left the house. The early morning sunlight peeked between the buildings as he hurried along the sidewalk toward the hotel. An occasional wagon clattered down the street, but the only people in sight were his fellow merchants as they prepared for the day's business. Too bad the wildflowers hadn't bloomed yet. Arriving with a bouquet of blossoms might raise his estimation in Miss Dalton's eyes.

He arrived at the hotel and tugged at his collar. Straightening his spine, he opened the door as the clock struck the quarter hour. Right on time. Attired in a sage-colored dress with lace at the collar and cuffs, Miss Dalton descended the stairs, a small reticule dangling from her wrist. A narrow-brimmed straw hat perched on her hair that had been pulled into a simple bun at the base of her head. A tentative smile clung to her lips, and he bowed as she approached. "Good morning. I hope the accommodations were acceptable."

"Yes, thank you." A slight pink colored her cheeks. "And thank you for escorting me this morning. I should have paid closer attention last night, because I don't think I could find the shop on my own."

"A lot has happened since you arrived." Flynn winked, and her blush deepened. He could get used to bringing roses to her face. He bent his arm. "But this is a new day, and I'm pleased to share it with you."

She slipped her hand into the crook of his elbow, and the warmth of her fingers sent a tremor to his shoulder as he led her out of the building. They sauntered toward the mercantile, and he gestured toward the various signs that swayed in the breeze, sharing stories about the folks who'd set up businesses in town. She nodded, and her brow furrowed as she repeated the names of his fellow shopkeepers. He stifled the urge to smooth the wrinkle from her forehead. How could he be affected by her nearness so soon after her arrival?

Flynn stopped in front of the mercantile and pulled the keys from his pocket. They jangled as he unlocked the door. He followed her inside and lit the lamps, the flickering flames pushing back the dimness. "There's a stockroom in the back where you can stow your bag, and an apron for you to put on to protect your outfit. I thought you could familiarize yourself with the inventory, then you can tell me if there are other items I should consider carrying, you know, for the ladies."

"But you don't know my taste." She pursed her lips. "What if I suggest something that doesn't sell? You would lose money."

"A risk I'm willing to take." He patted her arm. Thank goodness she didn't seem to be a spendthrift. "I appreciate your concern about the cost, but you're sure to know better about what women want." He guided her toward the curtain that hid the storage room from the customer space. "When you get inside, you'll see I've made more than a few poor choices."

She slipped past him into the storeroom, and he caught a whiff of lavender. Her eyes glowed, and she clapped her hands. "So many shelves of goodies."

Tension slid from his shoulders, and he chuckled. She liked his store, but what did she think about him?

Chapter Six

Surrounded by a half-dozen crates, Rayne fisted her hands on her hips and surveyed the shelves in the storeroom. Mr. Wade seemed to have as much product in the back as he did in the front of the shop. She didn't want to clutter the mercantile, but the more inventory the customers could browse, the more he'd sell. Her fingers itched to create sketches of possible displays, but first she needed to know what was in the most recent shipment. With his clerk's absence he'd been too busy to unpack the items and put them away.

A stray lock of hair had pulled from her bun, and she blew it out of her face. Mr. Wade had been in and out of the stockroom most of the morning, squeezing past her to reach for items. The last time he came in, he helped her dig through the excelsior to unload a lovely set of china. Several times their hands grazed as he passed her the delicate pieces to stack on the shelves, and tingles shot to her shoulder and wriggled down her back.

At well over six feet tall, he was the only man she'd ever had to look up to. Her own five-foot-ten-inch frame usually loomed over the men in her life, and none had been happy about the fact. His shirt stretched across his broad frame when he reached overhead, yet he moved with fluid grace rather than lumbering as others his size might do. A noise sounded behind her, and she bent into one of the crates to hide her heated face.

"Are you all right in here?" Mr. Wade's voice rumbled from the doorway. "The shop has been quite busy, but I'm sorry for leaving you alone."

Rayne took a deep breath and popped up, hoping her cheeks weren't as red as she feared. "Fine, just fine."

Concern pulsed from his steel-gray eyes, the color of the ocean on a cloudy day. "I don't want you to do too much on your first day of work."

She cocked her head and sent him a wry grin. "But it's okay to overwork beginning tomorrow?"

"What?" Confusion darkened his eyes, then they cleared as he chuckled. "Something like that." He gazed around the room. "You've made tremendous progress. It's nearly noon. Would you like to take a break for lunch?"

Her stomach gurgled, and she shrugged. "Apparently."

He threw his head back and laughed. "You are much less reticent in person, than you were in your letters. I like it."

Nibbling the inside of her cheek, Rayne twisted her mouth. She needed to be more like Jessica, but she kept forgetting. If too many of her own behaviors surfaced, he'd know something wasn't right. She and her sister were as different as black from white.

"I thought we could close the shop and eat our lunch." He held up a fragrant, towel-wrapped package. "How does that sound?"

"Perfect." She untied her apron and hung it on the hook by the door, then followed him out of the storeroom.

As they walked to the small table near the Franklin stove in the middle of the store, he rolled down his sleeves and buttoned his cuffs, his long tapered fingers making quick work of the task. He flipped the CLOSED sign, then held her chair as she sat. Handsome and courteous. No wonder her sister was willing to give up a life in Portland to move west and marry a stranger.

She blinked and licked her lips suddenly gone dry. What was wrong with her? No man had affected her like Flynn Wade, and certainly not within forty-eight hours of meeting.

While he unwrapped the cloth, then laid the food on her plate, he chatted about the folks she would meet at church and what she could expect from each little boy in Sunday school.

Rayne tucked her hands in her lap, this time ready for his prayer. She bit back a sigh as she bowed her head and waited for him to finish asking the blessing, as he called it. Did he ever talk about anything besides the business and God? She'd been too exhausted last night to open her sister's Bible, but she'd need to bone up before Sunday arrived or he'd discover her ignorance for sure.

Across the table, he smiled as he cut up the roasted chicken, his eyes crinkling at the corners. His teeth flashed against his dark, closely-trimmed beard. "I thought you were hungry." He pointed at her plate where she'd made trails in the potatoes.

Her face flamed, and she scooped some of the fluffy mixture into her mouth. Flavors exploded on her tongue, and her eyes widened.

"Delicious, right?" Mr. Wade winked. "René strikes again. He uses garlic and sage in his mash, and it's the best I've ever tasted."

"I could get used to him doing the cooking for us." She poked another forkful of potatoes into her mouth. "Truth be told, it's not my favorite task."

"Really?" He tugged at his ear. "From your letters, I thought you enjoyed creating new dishes."

Her stomach hollowed. She'd done it again—allowed her own personality and likes to overshadow Jessica's. "Well, uh...what I meant to say was I don't enjoy juggling making meals with my other responsibilities."

"Understandable." He nodded. "I've scheduled you to work until early afternoon in order for you to have the time to prepare dinner and handle the other tasks associated with running the house."

She took a sip of water to refrain from answering. How did she feel about him dictating the terms of her life? What hours she would spend on which duties? Had she exchanged one tedious job that paid for a volunteer position just as dreary? Her stomach roiled, and she pushed away her plate, the food no longer holding allure. She wiped her mouth on the linen napkin and rose. "I should get back to work. I'd like to make some preliminary sketches for your review."

He jumped to his feet. "Of course. I'll take care of clearing away the dishes."

"You're okay with doing that? Now that I'm here—"

"We'll share the duties." He grinned. "I've been a bachelor long enough to know how to wash up."

"All right." She edged past him, and her heel caught on the hem of her skirt. Her arms pinwheeled, and she stumbled against Mr. Wade's firm chest. His aroma of soap, bay rum, and his unique scent assailed her nose.

His arms went around her, and she regained her balance. Their faces inches apart, she could see tiny flecks of blue in his eyes. Her gaze went to his full lips, so close she could kiss them if she stood on tiptoe. Her pulse jumped as the air crackled between them. Did he feel the tension?

The bell on the door jangled behind her, and she sprang away from him, her face scorching. She ducked her head. "Thank you for preventing my fall. I didn't mean to be so clumsy. I'll get back to work." She peeked over her shoulder and cringed at the sight of Miss St. George standing with her hand on the knob.

Rayne swallowed past the lump in her throat, shoved aside the curtain, and rushed into the storeroom. Was the woman to be the bane of her existence? A constant reminder from Jessica's God that Rayne was here under pretense and had no right to marry Mr. Wade?

The curtain closed on the disappearing form of Miss Dalton, and Flynn finger-combed his hair, his palms still tingling from the feel of her. Why did Miss St. George have to show up now? Coincidence or the Lord preventing him from doing something foolish, like bending his head and pressing his lips to his betrothed's to see if they were as soft as they appeared?

His gaze swung from the storeroom door to his customer, and he forced a smile. "Miss St. George, nice to see you. How are you faring this morning?" He stopped short of asking her when she was leaving town. Hopefully, that bit of news was the reason for her visit.

She hesitated, then moved toward him. "I apologize for the intrusion, but I wanted to let you know I've come to the decision to remain in Rocky Mountains Springs for the time being."

"May I ask why?" He stuffed his hands into his pockets. "I don't want to come across as harsh, but I meant what I said when I indicated I can't marry you. Won't you feel awkward being here?"

"Please don't take this the wrong way, but I'm somewhat relieved we aren't to be wed." Her face pinked. "For the first time, I'm not under the watchful eyes of my parents, and I'd like to take advantage of the circumstances, see what I can become. Learn what I'm good at, other than doing needlepoint, serving tea, and discussing the latest fashions from London." She lifted one shoulder in a delicate shrug. "The little I've seen of America intrigues me, Mr. Wade. I'd like to discover more of life on my terms. You understand that, don't you?"

"Absolutely. I appreciate your candor." He grinned and pressed his hand against his chest in mock despair. "And I'll try not to be offended that you don't find me an acceptable mate."

Her color deepened. "You are most gracious." She giggled. "And a bit of a tease. Miss Dalton seems like a lovely woman. I have no intention of getting in the way of your relationship and hope you two will find true happiness." Her smile faltered. "However, I cannot remain at the hotel as a guest of your parents indefinitely. Would you help me find somewhere to stay, somewhat...uh...less expensive."

"Of course." He glanced over his shoulder. Miss Dalton was still out of sight. "I'd be happy to assist you. Most of the lodging choices are simple, dare I say it, rustic."

"You've managed to survive. I'd like to think I can as well." She smoothed her skirts. "There will be two of us. I've told my maid that's she's welcome to return to England, but she wants to share in the adventure."

"Even better." He rubbed his jaw. "There are two boarding houses in town that would be appropriate. They're each run by ladies from church and only cater to women. I believe they both have vacancies, and no matter which location you choose, you'll have a ready-made group of friends."

Her face lit, and the lines of tension cleared from her forehead. "Splendid. Would you be so kind as to write a letter of introduction for me?"

"I'll do you one better. How about if I escort you and provide a personal recommendation?"

Footsteps approached from behind.

Miss Dalton stood next to the counter, her reticule clutched between tight fingers and a deep frown on her face. Her piercing gaze bounced from him to Miss St. George. "I'm finished for the day."

Flynn swallowed a sigh. He might not know a lot about women, but everything in Miss Dalton's stance told him she was not happy, perhaps even jealous. How much of the conversation had she heard? Was his prospective bride as temperamental as she was beautiful?

Chapter Seven

Sunlight streamed through the window as Rayne curled up on her bed and flipped through her sketchbook. Three days had passed since she'd fallen into Flynn's arms in front of Miss St. George. Three days of awkward togetherness in the mercantile. He'd informed her of the English woman's plans, during dinner that evening, and Rayne's hope that her competition would return from whence she came disappeared in an instant.

Her gaze returned to the drawings, and she smiled. No matter what happened between her and Flynn—he was no longer Mr. Wade, not after their *encounter*—she loved the little town of Rocky Mountain Springs. Warm and friendly, the inhabitants greeted her as if she was one of them. Many came to the shop specifically to introduce themselves and welcome her as if they cared. Even her coworkers at the cannery hadn't been that interested in her life, and they'd worked side by side for nearly five years.

She blew out a sigh and tossed aside the book, then climbed to her feet. She rubbed her damp palms on her skirt and paced. A quick glance at the watch pinned to her bodice told her that Flynn would arrive to escort her to church in a few minutes. As soon as she arrived at the sanctuary, she'd be doomed. He'd discover her subterfuge, discover the ugly truth that she was not a believer, which would topple the house of cards she'd built by taking Jessica's identity.

Having been dragged to services on Christmas and Easter by her sister, she wasn't totally ignorant in the ways of the church, but would her experience be enough? She avoided looking at her reflection in the mirror. *Her* face, not Jessica's. What had she been thinking when she decided to come to Wyoming in her sister's stead? She frowned and continued to pace. The truth was she'd had no choice, but Flynn didn't deserve to get hurt in the bargain.

Perhaps she should feign illness or fatigue. She could claim a migraine. Her stomach hollowed. No. She didn't need to compound her deceit with further lying. Besides, she'd eventually have to attend services, and the sooner the better. At least he'd called off Sunday school with the boys for her first week.

The door rattled with a knock, and she startled. "Yes?"

"Miss Dalton, Mr. Wade is downstairs for you."

"I'll be right there." Her mouth went dry, and she poured water from the pitcher into one of the glasses. Drinking deeply, she closed her eyes, then set down the glass and pressed a hand against her thumping heart. "You can do this. You must."

Rayne picked up her wrap and reticule, then headed out of the room. She snapped her fingers, went back inside, and grabbed Jessica's Bible. Was it her imagination, or did the leather cover feel warm to the touch? Would it burst into flames as judgment for her behaviors? She gulped and shut the door before she could change her mind and leave the book behind. She trudged down the hall and descended into the lobby where Flynn waited.

Dressed in a navy-blue suit that fit him as if hand tailored, his gray eyes twinkled as he smiled. His white shirt was starched and ironed, with a paisley blue and green tie knotted at the neck. He bowed, then took her hand and tucked it in the crook of his elbow. "You look lovely this morning, Miss Dalton."

"Thank you." She trembled. Fortunately, he didn't use her first name or, rather, Jessica's name, when he spoke to her. Apparently, he still carried some of his social customs from England which suited her just fine. Would she ever get used to responding to her sister's name?

They left the hotel and walked to the church, joining others who sauntered toward the white clapboard structure, its bell pealing a loud greeting. Wagons filled with families and couples clattered down the street, then parked in the field adjacent to the building.

Flynn led her inside, and she waved to the few people she recognized. Her neck prickled as she received more than a few stares and studied looks. Now, she knew how a bug felt under one of those microscopes she'd read about. She raised her chin and straightened her spine. She wouldn't let them see her nerves.

He gestured to a nearby pew, and she sat down. He settled beside her and winked before picking up a slim hardback volume. He paged through it, and she cringed. A hymnal. She forgot about all the singing that occurred during a church service. She leaned toward him and whispered, "I think it's best I just read along. I hope you understand."

"God only expects us to make a joyful noise, but it's your decision." He smiled. "Are you really that bad?"

"Yes, but I don't plan to prove it today."

The service started, and after several excruciating minutes of congregational singing, the pastor stepped to the pulpit. "Good morning, everyone. I like to extend a special welcome to Miss Jessica Dalton, who has joined our community from Portland, Maine. She is Flynn Wade's betrothed, so be sure to greet her after the service."

A smattering of applause filled the sanctuary, and Rayne forced a smile. Perspiration pooled under her arms. Beside her, Flynn lifted his hand and grinned, his shoulder bumping hers and sending tingles to her wrist.

Silence descended, and the preacher held up his Bible. "This morning, I'd like to share a few thoughts from Jesus' sermon on the mount. Known as the beatitudes, these verses in the fifth chapter of Matthew's gospel speak to us about our...well, attitudes."

A chuckle swept over the crowd. Rayne fidgeted. Apparently, this church was going to be like every other one she'd attended—a man in front pointing out all the bad things she'd done and making her feel worthless. She bit back a sigh and crossed her arms.

"Friends, these are powerful words spoken by our Lord, 'Blessed are the poor in spirit: for theirs is the kingdom of heaven. Blessed are they that mourn: for they shall be comforted. Blessed are the meek: for they shall inherit the earth. Blessed are they which do hunger and thirst after righteousness: for they shall be filled.'"

He smiled and cradled his Bible close to his chest. "Doesn't that give you hope? Don't His words grab you to the core. He feels your pain and suffering. Jesus knows exactly what you're going through and wants to give you His fullness. An abundant life you can only find in Him."

Rayne's jaw dropped, and tears pricked the backs of her eyes. He mourned with her? He cared about her sadness? Her despair? Surely, not someone like her. The pastor must be talking to the other people in the audience, those who came regularly.

"Do you have burdens on your heart, beloved?" The preacher's forehead wrinkled. "Most of us do. God wants us to turn over our anxieties to Him so He can carry them for you. No hardship is too large or too inconsequential." His eyes seemed to be riveted on Rayne's face. "I'm speaking to each and every one of you today."

Mesmerized by the man's words, Rayne swallowed the lump in her throat. Jessica had tried to tell her of God's love, but Rayne had scoffed at the concept. And now Jessica was dead. If God cared for her, why did He take her sister? He was the One who created the mourning, the burden. And the Bible said He was willing to take them back. Hardly.

She shifted in the hard pew. After church, she should confess what she'd done and board the first train out of town. Or maybe she'd just tell Flynn she'd changed her mind. He didn't need to know the truth. Did he?

Pastor Taggart's words washed over Flynn like a warm blanket. The beatitudes were some of his favorite verses. When life got difficult, he'd drag out his Bible and read the chapter as a reminder that God knew exactly what he was dealing with.

Flynn glanced at Miss Dalton from the corner of his eye. She seemed to be immersed in the sermon which was a relief. When he met her at the hotel, she seemed hesitant, almost adverse, to accompanying him to church. After he'd asked if she felt well enough to attend, she'd assured him she was perfectly fine. However, the doubt clouding her eyes and the lines bracketing her mouth told a different story.

Did she regret leaving Portland? Did she think his congregation tiny compared to the one she'd left? While living in the large coastal town, she had her choice of churches, most with huge gatherings and highly educated, erudite speakers. Rocky Mountain Springs First Baptist's little collection of believers would probably fit in the choir loft of her last church.

A self-taught man, Pastor Taggart had come to Wyoming in one of the first wagon trains on the Oregon Trail after he felt called to tame the West through God's Word. His sermons were simple, yet heartfelt, and always struck a chord with Flynn. He could count on some kernel of wisdom to surface by the end of the service. Would Miss Dalton feel the same way?

He looked forward to discussing her thoughts about the sermon over lunch. They'd touched on their mutual faith in the few letters they'd exchanged but had refrained from extensive conversations. He'd asked her enough questions to ensure she was truly a believer rather than one of those women he'd heard about, who pretended to be someone they weren't to get free passage out West, and her answers had convinced him of her authenticity.

Seeing her engrossed in the homily, he sat up straighter. She clung to every word that came from the pastor's mouth, yet Flynn was woolgathering and thinking about his prospective bride rather than the Lord. His face burned. She was obviously the more spiritual of the two of them. He'd have to spend more time on the Scriptures to grow into the kind of husband who could lead his family. God had surely shown him favor by providing her.

"Blessed are the pure in heart, for they shall see God," the pastor's voice rumbled. "Blessed are the peacemakers, for they shall be called the children of God. Isn't that wonderful?"

Flynn smiled and glanced at Miss Dalton, as beautiful on the outside as she seemed to be on the inside. Movement past her caught his eye, and his gaze flicked to Miss St. George seated a couple of pews ahead.

Wearing another stylish silk gown and hat, she looked in his direction, a serene smile on her face. She, too, seemed to be receiving encouragement from the pastor's words. He squared his shoulders and returned her smile. Her eyes lit, and she dipped her head in acknowledgment.

Miss Dalton slanted a look at him, then followed his gaze. Turning back, she narrowed her eyes, pinning him to the pew with a piercing glare. Her mouth thinned into a slash, and she crossed her arms.

He winced. He'd have a lot of explaining to do after the service. Would she believe he'd meant nothing by his smile at Miss St. George?

Chapter Eight

Behind the counter at the mercantile, Flynn assisted the Delaney sisters with their purchases while Miss Dalton worked on a display that combined cookware, dinnerware, and canned goods. She called it cross merchandising and said she'd seen it done in the Boston department stores. The idea was that people would see products used together prompting them to purchase the entire lot. Her new displays were highly successful, and the shop's revenue had jumped significantly. She'd even managed to create a display that made the hideous lamps look attractive, and all but one had been sold.

Two weeks had passed since the incident in church when he'd made the mistake of smiling at Miss St. George across the sanctuary. He'd apologized profusely, and they'd come to an uneasy truce with Miss Dalton seeming to believe that he was only being friendly to the English woman. He'd told her about the distrust and wariness he'd experienced when he opened the shop, and he didn't want her to suffer the same fate.

Mrs. Harrison, a difficult woman who criticized everything, approached Miss Dalton, and Flynn held his breath. Despite being a foot shorter than her, the elderly woman still managed to look down her nose while speaking. He could hear her strident tones but not her words. Should he go over and rescue Miss Dalton?

With one eye on Mrs. Harrison, he handed the paper-wrapped packaged to the Delaney sisters. "Have a lovely day, ladies. Thank you for shopping with us."

Ethel, the outspoken one of the pair, smiled and shot a look over her shoulder. "We wouldn't dream of going anywhere else, Mr. Wade. You have the best selection and quality in all of Wyoming." Her voice was louder than usual, and he swallowed a grin. It seemed the old gal was trying to let the widow know not everyone shared her opinion.

"Again, thank you." He bowed and led them to the door that he held open for them.

"Such a gentleman, Mr. Wade." Ethel looped arms with her sister and winked. "I hope your young lady realizes what a good catch you are."

Flynn gaped at her, but before he could respond, the pair strolled out the door huddled together and chatting between themselves. He chuckled and shook his head, then returned to the shop. Laughter came from behind the knitting display, and he lifted one eyebrow as he strode toward the sound. Rounding the shelves, he stopped short.

Miss Dalton and Mrs. Harrison stood close together, broad smiles on both their faces. How had his bride-to-be manage to amuse the demanding and often crotchety woman? Had he ever seen her smile? He'd surely never seen her laugh.

"Can I help you, Mr. Wade?" Miss Dalton looked at him with wariness. "Did you need something?"

"Uh...no, just...uh...headed to the storeroom and wanted to let you know." He tugged at his collar. "I won't be but a few minutes."

"Okay. I'll hold down the fort." She picked up one of the skeins of yarn and handed it to Mrs. Harrison. "The particular color would suit you perfectly. It brings out the roses in your cheeks."

The woman touched her face. "You think so? I've always loved this particular shade of pink."

Flynn hurried to the stockroom to keep from staring at the two of them and making a further fool of himself. How had Miss Dalton broken through Mrs. Harrison's veneer of haughtiness? His face warmed. And why hadn't he made an attempt? Instead, he was cold and standoffish, doing whatever he could to hurry her transaction and get her out of the store. *Forgive me, Lord. It appears I'm going to learn a thing or two from my fiancée about how to treat others.*

Moments later, he left the stockroom, and Miss Dalton looked at him from behind the counter. The clock on the shelf near the door chimed five o'clock, and he made a detour to the door, then flipped the CLOSED sign. He forked his fingers through his hair. "Another good day. You worked wonders with Mrs. Harrison."

A flush covered her cheeks, and she shrugged. "You've got to meet people where they are, and she's lonely. Her husband died a few years ago, and what others see as snootiness is shyness. He's no longer around to make her feel cherished. People need to feel special."

"Very astute of you for understanding. I'm embarrassed to admit I've hurried her from the shop to avoid the sharp side of her tongue." He bounced on his toes. "You're a good woman, Miss Dalton. Would you like to take a walk before heading home?"

"That would be lovely."

"If you'll give me a hand balancing the drawer, we can be on our way in a shake."

She nodded and perched on one of the stools, then grabbed the stack of receipts and reached past him for a pencil.

The crisp scent of lavender wafted passed him, and his pulse skittered. He opened the cash drawer, then gave himself a mental slap. Focus, man. He made quick work of counting the money while she tallied the sales. She showed him the figure at the bottom of the last receipt, and his eyes widened, then he grinned. "I believe that's the best day I've had since opening. Perhaps you should be in charge of the store."

A shadow flitted across her face. "No, thank you. I had enough of worrying about money in Portland. I'll stick to playing with the merchandise."

"I'm sorry to bring up bad memories." He cocked his head. "How is your sister faring? We should bring her here."

"No, she's...uh...no." An emotion he couldn't decipher clouded her eyes. She handed him the receipts and hopped off the stool. "I'm ready for that walk." She pulled her satchel from under the counter, and a large book of some sort fell to the floor. The cover flipped open to reveal a pencil sketch of him before she slammed it shut and tried to stuff the book into her bag.

He grabbed the volume and tugged. "Let me see that."

Her face flamed to the roots of her hair. "No, I'm not very good."

"I beg to differ. The face on the page was me, wasn't it?"

She continued to grip the book and refused to meet his eyes. "Yes. I'm sorry. I shouldn't have drawn your picture without asking."

"Permission isn't necessary." He stifled a grin. She must feel something for him if she spent time putting his likeness on paper. How many more renditions were there? He yanked the book from her hands.

Her face fell, and she hunched into herself. "I'd rather you didn't look."

Flynn returned the sketchbook, the sadness on her face filling him with remorse. "Of course." He handed her the volume. "I was teasing and didn't mean to upset you."

Shoving the book into her bag, she scooted from behind the counter.

His throat thickened. What a dunce he was to put her on the spot. In a flash, he struck a pose like a strong man in the circus, flexing his arms on either side of his head. "How's this? You can draw me like this." He put his hands on his hips and crouched. "Or this." Putting his index finger and thumb together on each hand, he held them to his eyes like spectacles. "Or how about this."

The darkness on her cheeks lifted, and she giggled.

His chest lightened, and he grabbed his hat from the hook, plunked it on his head, and grabbed his vest lapels. Thrusting out his chin, he squared his shoulders. "Much better, right?"

"Without a doubt." She laughed, and she returned to his side, then grasped his hat and tilted it on his head. "Now, we're talking. You look like a man about town."

"A proper gentleman, eh?"

She nodded, her eyes sparkling in the light of the lamp. "Too bad we don't have a blossom for your buttonhole."

"No, then I'd look like a dandy."

Forming a square with her fingers, she held up her hand as if to frame him. She stepped forward and tripped on the stool, tumbling toward him.

His arms went around her, and the clean scent of her hair assailed him. Her face tilted toward his, and her pupils dilated. His breath caught. Her mouth was close, close enough to kiss if he lowered his head just a fraction. Dare he press his lips to hers?

Chapter Nine

Heart pounding against her ribs, Rayne stared into Flynn's eyes. His breath brushed her cheek like a feather, soft and gentle. Arms around her in a firm embrace, his hands were warm through the thin fabric of her dress. Did he realize he was drawing lazy circles on her back as they stared at each other?

Rayne shivered at his touch. He towered over her making her feel petite and feminine, foreign emotions that left her unsettled. His pupils dilated, the gray becoming a thin circle, and his eyes searched hers, probing, questioning. She licked her lips, and his gaze moved to her mouth.

Her arms snaked around his waist, and her pulse skittered. What was she doing? Yes, they were technically betrothed, but thus far their relationship had been a series of fits and starts. More awkward than easygoing moments. Was she ready for this next step?

He lowered his head. The air between them crackled. His lips brushed hers, his beard tickling her skin.

She hiccupped. Not a sweet, quiet peep, but a spasmodic gasp that sounded like a pig squealing. Her face burned. She'd once again proven herself a bumbling, ungraceful girl.

Flynn yanked back, his mouth set in a perfect O. His eyebrows shot up to his hairline, and he dropped his arms. He cleared his throat, then raked his fingers through his hair, a gesture that seemed to be his habit when he was unsure.

Stepping back, she rubbed her arms. "Well, thank you for preventing my fall. Very gallant of you." Another hiccup erupted from inside her, and she clamped her lips. A nervous giggle forced its way out, then she snickered and covered her face with cold hands.

He chuckled and tucked a stray hair behind her ear. "It's nothing to be embarrassed about."

She peeked between her fingers. "Says you." She shrugged and gave in to her laughter.

One eyelid lowered in a slow wink, and he grinned. "That's one way to break a moment."

Before she could respond, a knock sounded at the door, and he sighed. "These last few days, I've done more business after hours than I imagined possible." He marched to the door and flicked open the lock.

Rayne gulped. With any luck the person outside hadn't seen them through the window. She patted her hair, then straightened her spine. And hopefully, she didn't look as disheveled as she felt. Crossing her arms, she forced a smile as the sheriff walked in. A chill swept over her. Had he somehow gotten word about who she was? "Good evening, Sheriff," she spoke through wooden lips.

"Evening, young lady. Sorry to bother you folks, but we've run out of coffee at the jail, and it promises to be a long night. Me and the deputies just rounded up a gang of ruffians at the Double J ranch doing some cattle rustling, so we need to keep our wits about us. No telling if they'll try to escape."

Her hands flew to her throat. "Are they dangerous?"

He pushed his Stetson back on his head. "They sure are. There's big money to be made stealing livestock, and they won't want to spend even one night behind bars." He rotated his shoulders. "And they didn't come easy, but my boys did a good job."

She exchanged a look with Flynn. Would she be safe at the hotel? What had she gotten herself into by leaving the civilized streets of Portland for the wilds of Wyoming?

"Nothing for you to worry about Je—Miss Dalton. The last thing these guys will do if they escape is hang around town and frequent the hotel. But after we're done here, I'll walk you home, and you should retire to your room for the rest of the night."

"Th-thank you." She wrung her hands, then stuffed them into the pockets of her dress.

Flynn walked to the tins where he stored the coffee and grabbed a canvas sack from the shelf. He popped the lid on the canister and scooped several cups of beans into the bag. He held up the pouch. "That enough for you, Sheriff?"

The lanky man nodded. "Should be plenty." He pulled out his wallet.

"It's on the house." Flynn shook his head as he handed the lawman his purchase. "Nice to know you're keeping us safe. The least I can do is help keep you and the lads awake."

"Thank you kindly." He touched the brim of his hat and left the mercantile, the door swinging closed behind him with a thud.

"Let me put the deposit in the safe and we'll head out now. I'm sorry to forego our stroll, but I think it's for the best." He disappeared into the storeroom.

"All right." She touched her mouth. Would he say anything about their almost kiss on the way to the hotel, or would his proper English upbringing ensure he avoided the topic? Her lips tingled. Her first kiss, but the gesture barely qualified as such. Even so, her lips ached for more.

She closed her eyes. Whether she liked it or not, she'd begun to care for Flynn Wade. He was a handsome man, but she was drawn to his gentle, caring nature and razor-sharp sense of humor. No, it was more than that. She was falling for him, hard.

Did he feel the same way? Is that why he'd tried to kiss her? Or was he just caught up in the moment?

Her stomach hollowed. Their relationship would never be real as long as he thought he was in love with Jessica. The sweet, honest, God-fearing twin. Not Rayne.

What would he do if she confessed her deceit? Put her on the next train out of town? Have her arrested? Her heart jumped to her throat at the idea of sitting in a cell next to a bunch of menacing cattle robbers. Should she come clean, or would her admission cause more harm than good?

The pastor's words from Sunday's sermon leapt to her mind. "There is no sin too great that our Lord can't forgive."

God might forgive her, but what about Flynn?

Chapter Ten

Overcast and dreary, the afternoon sky was filled with swollen, black clouds. Rayne immersed herself in arranging a display of gardening supplies while Flynn puttered on the other side of the store putting away the sacks of feed that had arrived on the morning train. The train that kept tempting her to flee before either of them got hurt. Normally decisive, she continued to waffle about what to do.

Last night after he'd walked her home, and she'd locked herself in the hotel room, she'd tossed and turned for hours reliving the not-quite-a-kiss and considering her options—confess her lie, cut out and run, or continue the subterfuge. Every time she determined the best course of action being to maintain the ruse, Pastor Taggart's sermons would edge into her mind, and guilt would prick her conscience. She'd roll over, punch the pillow, and commence arguing with herself again.

She blew out a sigh and tucked seed packets in a willow-twig basket she'd lined with a bit of fabric. Next, she tied a ribbon around a small pail and filled the bucket with hand tools to mimic a bouquet. Her gaze fell on the trowel, and her mouth twisted. She'd certainly dug a hole for herself, and every day that passed, the hole got a bit bigger.

The bell on the door rang, and heavy footsteps clomped into the shop. She peeked around the shelves and gasped, then clapped a hand over her mouth. Not four feet away stood Mr. Biggs, a manager from the cannery, this one even more despicable than Mr. Cross, who tended to be grumpy, whereas this man had a mean streak a mile wide. He'd walk the floors deriding the workers, and he seemed to take particular pleasure in alternating between lambasting the women and making lewd comments. More than once he'd intimated that the gals could get better jobs if they became *friends* with him.

A shiver crawled up her spine, and she swallowed the bile that rose in her throat. What was he doing here? Had he followed her? Maybe his appearance was pure coincidence. Maybe he wouldn't recognize her. She rolled her eyes. Yeah, and maybe she'd look outside and see cows flying.

From the back of the shop, Flynn called, "Jess—Miss Dalton, can you take care of our guest?"

"Will do." She grimaced. Flynn had almost called her Jessica. She wiped her damp palms on her skirt and climbed to her feet. Forcing a smile, she approached Mr. Biggs. "Good afternoon, sir, and welcome to our store. How may we be of service?"

The man leered at her, his gaze raking her from head to toe. His eyes narrowed, and he cocked his head. "Is this the only mercantile in this one-horse town?"

"No, sir, but we are the largest, and dare I say it, have the best selection." She forced a smile. "And if we don't have what you need, we can order the items."

His neck swiveled as he surveyed the store. "You do have a decent amount of stuff in here." He turned back toward her, studying her face for a long moment. "Guess I'll look around for a bit and let you know if I need help, honey."

"Take your time, and Mr. Wade or I can answer any questions you may have."

"I much prefer getting help from you, little lady." He winked and squeezed her shoulder. "I'll let you know when I'm ready." He pivoted on his heel.

Nausea swept over her, and her stomach hollowed. She shuddered and resisted the urge to wipe away the feel of his hand. He hadn't seemed to recognize her, but apparently he treated all women with disdain, not just those under his purview at the factory. Was he in Wyoming for personal reasons, or had the company seen fit to send the loathsome man on some sort of business trip? Why would they want such a contemptible person to represent them?

"You've got most of what I need to set up my office, but I will have to order a few things."

She whirled at the sound of Mr. Biggs's voice in her ear. She'd been so engrossed with worry, she'd failed to hear his approach. Her heart dropped. He was staying? The town was not large enough for her to avoid him, especially if Flynn's mercantile was the man's shop of choice. "You have business here?"

He tucked his thumbs in his belt and rocked on his heels. "Yep, my company's considering building a meat packing plant here, and they sent me to do some reconnaissance. In my opinion this place is way too small, but maybe the factory will bring 'em in." He shrugged. "I get paid no matter what happens, so makes no nevermind to me."

"A factory?" She stiffened. No doubt just as bleak and dangerous as the cannery. If she wanted to thwart his plans, she needed to know more. She fluttered her eyelashes like she'd seen some of the girls do. "You must be very smart for your employer to send you here for such an important job. I'd be happy to help you requisition the items not in stock."

He leaned close. "Are you? Or are you just saying that, Miss Dalton?"

"I'm sorry?"

"I finally figured out why you look familiar. You used to work at the cannery, and I don't remember you being this amenable. In fact, you were a bit of a troublemaker, always complaining, always telling us what we should be doing for the workers." His arms gestured to the shelves. "You've got yourself a sweet setup here. Not sure how you managed it or what you told this guy to hire you, but your secret is safe with me. For now."

She drew herself up to her full height. "I assure you, Mr. Biggs, there is no secret. Mr. Wade is fully aware of my history at the cannery."

Maybe so, *Rayne,* but I'm pretty sure he thinks you're Jessica. I heard what he said when he asked you to give me a hand." He sneered and jabbed her with his elbow. "Is it money you're after? Does your fancy British boss have a title you want? Must have taken a lot of planning to get yourself out here. I'm impressed."

"I don't know what you're talking about." Could the man hear the tremor in her voice? "I'm Jessica Dalton, and yes, I used to work for you, but that's the end of my story."

"Did you really think I wouldn't remember that Jessica died? I had to fill out reams of paper, and the state swooped in to investigate her death. Days of interviews and meetings. Fortunately, they finally came to the realization we'd done nothing wrong, and it was her own fault she got hurt." His face darkened, and he pointed his finger at her. "But the debacle set us back weeks on production. I suggest you watch yourself, missy, because I may just need to share your little secret with your boss."

"Is there a problem here?"

Rayne's head whipped around.

Flynn approached from behind a set of shelves. Had he heard their exchange? If not, would Mr. Biggs reveal her identity to watch her squirm? Her web of lies was getting more tangled.

Tension clung to the air like a wet blanket as Flynn approached Miss Dalton, her body thrumming like a plucked guitar string. His gaze fell on the weasel-like man with beady eyes, and he was glad to loom over the customer who'd obviously upset her. "Good afternoon, sir. Is there something I can assist you with?"

Flynn had to give the man credit for not giving ground. Instead, he squared his shoulders, puffed out his chest, and said, "I'm here as a representative of Baker and Sons. I'm sure you've heard of us. We own canneries, factories, and meat packing plants, which means I've got lots of money to spend. Your girl here was doing just fine. We were...uh...just getting acquainted. Seems she's new in town, too."

"Yes, sir, which is why I should perhaps give you a hand instead. The mercantile is mine, so I'm fully versed on our products and would be able to offer attractive pricing." Flynn peeked at Miss Dalton. Her body taut, her expression was a mixture of disgust and fear. Fear? Had the man threatened her, or had his references to canneries provoked a terrible memory? He touched Miss Dalton's arm, and she blinked. "The garden display is coming together beautifully. Would you like to finish it while I assist Mr. Biggs?"

Her breath whooshed out as if she'd been holding it too long, and she nodded. She dipped her head to the customer. "Would you please excuse me? It was a...uh...nice to meet you."

"Yeah, you too." The man watched her walk away, then turned and winked at Flynn. "Must be nice to work with that every day."

Flynn gritted his teeth. The man was pompous, condescending, and uncouth. No amount of income was worth dealing with someone like him, especially with his attitude and comments about Jessica. "Sir, Miss Dalton is my fiancée, and I'd appreciate it if you refrain from making inappropriate comments about her."

"No need to get your knickers in a twist." Mr. Biggs grinned. "You Brits are too provincial. Here in America we don't hesitate to speak our mind. I was just appreciating her beauty. I didn't mean any offense."

"What you call provincial, I consider good manners, as will most of the folks in our town."

"You're able to speak on everyone's behalf, are you?" Biggs's face darkened. "Who put you in charge? What's the real reason you're in America? Couldn't make it on your own in merry old England? Running from something?"

Flynn clenched his fists and stifled the urge to knock the smirk off the man's face with a punch. Instead, he gripped Biggs's arm and dragged him to the front door. "I believe you would be happier shopping elsewhere, sir, but thank you for stopping by."

"You're going to be sorry you crossed me, Wade. I'm going to do great things for this cow town, and they won't include you and your sorry excuse for a store." He tore his arm from Flynn's grasp and yanked open the door. "And you might want to find out what you can about that cute clerk of yours." He marched outside and slammed the door, the bell ringing in protest.

Scrubbing at his face with cold fingers, Flynn groaned. Would he rue making an enemy of the abhorrent runt?

"Thank you, Mr. Wade."

He turned.

Miss Dalton stood behind him wringing her hands, her face ashen. "I'm sorry you'll lose business because of me. I'm not sure how things managed to get out of hand so quickly. I've dealt with his type before, and the situation usually rights itself."

"He's a disagreeable little man whose behaviors have been allowed to happen. I will not serve someone who insults those I care about." He cupped her jaw in his hand, and her eyes widened. "God will take care of our finances, and even if He doesn't, I won't compromise my stand."

She averted her gaze and moved out of reach, her arms wrapped around her waist. "If you say so, but I hope the incident won't cause you problems." Her face brightened. "I do appreciate you coming to my rescue. No one's ever done that before."

He smiled and bowed, relieved to see the haunted look disappear from her eyes. "I'm happy to do so, m'lady."

Chapter Eleven

Laughter punctuated the air as children chased each other across the church lawn. The men brought chairs from inside the building while the women chatted and arranged their dishes on the tables. Commotion swirled around Rayne as she poked serving utensils into the food, feeling like the fifth wheel on a wagon. Because she was in no position to cook at the hotel, Flynn had brought their contribution made by his housekeeper.

Next to her, Yvonne smiled and brushed a stray hair out of her face with the back of her hand. "We couldn't have asked for a prettier day to hold the potluck." She jerked her head toward Flynn who was laying out blankets under one of the trees, a broad grin on his face. "I'm glad you're here. I've never seen Flynn this happy."

Rayne's face warmed, and she shrugged. "He's a nice man. I'm honored he selected me as his bride."

Yvonne nudged her shoulder. "From the color of your cheeks, I'd say you're more than honored, and I'm pleased. Not all the mail-order marriages work out."

"Really?" Guilt nipped her. "Why not?"

"Lots of reasons. Sometimes expectations aren't met. Other times one partner or the other isn't who they seem. And in a few cases, the husband turns out to be a bully, if you know what I mean, and the gal is smart enough to flee."

Eyes wide, Rayne gaped at the woman. "That's terrible."

"Yes, but fortunately I don't think that sort of thing happens often." She unwrapped a platter of biscuits. "But you don't have to worry about Flynn. He's a kind, gentle soul, willing to give the shirt off his back to help others in need. In fact, he won't admit it, but he's been known to leave food and supplies on the porches of those who are struggling. He usually makes the drop early in the morning so he won't be seen, but a few of us have caught him in the act. We let him think he's getting away with something. And last year, he bought a bunch of Bibles for the church because most folks can't afford them. "

"I had no idea." Rayne cocked her head. Flynn looked up and met her gaze. Her pulse skipped. "He hasn't told me about that or asked for my assistance. I guess he's still keeping it a secret."

"Maybe I spoke out of turn." Yvonne dipped her head and rearranged a couple of bowls.

"No, I'm glad to know. And I'm sure he'll tell me when the time is right. We're still getting acquainted." Rayne tugged at her collar as sunshine heated her back. One more person confirming what she already knew about her prospective groom: he was a gracious Christian man who deserved an honest, Christian wife who could serve by his side. And she wasn't that woman.

Tears welled, and she blinked them away. "Excuse me. I'm going to see if there's anything else that needs to be brought outside." She marched toward the church, threading her way through the milling crowd, then trotted up the steps and into the building. The door closed behind her, and she hesitated to let her eyes adjust to the dimness.

Silence enveloped her, and she wandered toward the front of the sanctuary, her footsteps echoing on the wood floor. She spied Pastor Taggart's Bible on the first pew. What would he say about her deceit? He preached forgiveness. Would he bestow it if she asked? If she told him what she'd done, would he be required to maintain her secret like the priests in the Catholic church? Did she want him to?

Rayne lowered herself onto the bottom step leading to the altar. She'd been in Wyoming less than a month, and she was already exhausted from living a lie. What would it be like six months from now, or a lifetime? Flynn deserved to know the truth. Which confession would hit him the hardest? That she wasn't her sister or that she wasn't a believer? Could he forgive either or both falsehoods?

Pastor Taggart's voice drifted through the open window. "Gather round, everyone. It's time to say the blessing before we dig into this sumptuous feast."

Her stomach tightened. Even if she wished to change, God wouldn't want her. She'd done too many bad things. Could she ever be worthy of Him? A powerful Being, He probably only loved people like Flynn or Jessica. Men and women who did good deeds and had pure thoughts. Not like her, who lost her temper, lied, cheated, stole. The list was endless.

She bowed her head. Why did she continue to remain in Rocky Mountain Springs? During her many sleepless nights, she'd convinced herself to pack up, leave, and skedaddle before she hurt Flynn any further. Then morning would arrive, and she'd tell herself that one more day would be okay. If she left now, he wouldn't be as upset. He'd recover, find a nice girl to love him. Mrs. Crenshaw could rustle up a bride. One who would be much better suited and be deserving of Flynn's love.

Love.

She touched her lips, the memory of the feel of his mouth on hers, curling her toes. She might not love him, not after only three weeks, but she sure liked him. A lot.

The door opened, and a slash of light puddled in the aisle. "Miss Dalton?" Flynn stepped forward. "Jess—Miss Dalton. Are you in here?"

Rayne climbed to her feet. "Yes."

He hurried forward, a deep crease in his forehead. "Are you ill? I can take you home...well, back to the hotel."

She forced a smile and straightened her spine. "I'm fine. I...uh...came in to retrieve things for the potluck, but it appears I'm too late. Then I got to thinking. I'm sorry to make you worry."

"Are you homesick? Missing your sister?"

A lump formed in her throat, threatening to choke her. She swallowed and nodded. At least she could give him an honest answer this time.

"I can't make you miss her less, but perhaps I can chase away some of your sadness. I have something for you." He pulled a package bound in brown paper and twine from behind his back. "I hope you like it."

"A gift?" Her voice broke, and she cleared her throat. "Why bring it to the potluck?"

He lifted one of his shoulders. "I often think of my family during special events, and I anticipated that might happen to you making today difficult." He gestured to a nearby pew. "Come, sit with me."

Her chin trembled as she sat, and she untied the knot. The wrapper fell away exposing a leather-bound sheaf of drawing paper and set of pencils. Her jaw dropped. Tears pricked the backs of her eyes, then tumbled down her cheeks. She stroked the soft buttery cover. "Why?"

His face shone. "When your book fell the other day, I noticed you only had a few more blank pages."

"But pencils, too. This is expensive. I can't accept it." She tried to return the book, but he held up his hands.

"Of course you can accept this. We're to be married, and I reserve the right to shower you with presents."

Rayne cried harder and jumped to her feet. Cradling the gift to her chest, she ran down the aisle and pushed open the door. She clattered down the steps and ducked her head to prevent seeing the staring faces of the congregation. Lifting her skirts with one hand, she raced down the walkway toward the hotel. Why did Flynn have to be so perfect?

Chapter Twelve

The door closed with a bang, and Flynn stared slack-jawed at the spot where Miss Dalton had been standing. How had the moment soured in the blink of an eye? What about the gift had upset her? Since her arrival she'd been hesitant to accept his payment for items, but perhaps that came from having to provide for herself in Portland. Having to be independent through no fault of her own. But this reaction seemed different, almost despairing.

He rubbed his forehead and blew out a sigh. Should he follow her? Over the last few days, their conversations had been open, even candid at times. Would she be willing to discuss what troubled her, or should he leave her to her own devices? *Now what, Lord?*

The door opened, and sunlight splashed inside. Alonzo stepped into the sanctuary, Yvonne close at his heels. He wore a dark glare. "What did you do? Miss Dalton seemed agitated."

Flynn held up his hands as in surrender. "I presented her with a gift...drawing paper and pencils. She said the items cost too much, and she couldn't accept them. I pressed my point, and she began to cry." He scuffed his shoe on the floor. "And as you saw, they weren't happy tears, more like grief. I don't know what to do."

Alonzo clapped him on the shoulder. "Be patient, my friend. A woman's emotions can be fragile things. Like those bone china cups you sell. In the wrong hands, they can break. In this case, I think you need to keep your big mitts off the situation. Just for a bit. Give her some space to get control of herself."

"Is that true, Yvonne?" Flynn's gaze flicked to his friend's wife. "Should I leave her alone for the time being? She won't think I'm ignoring her and her feelings?"

Yvonne smiled and nudged her husband. "This man of mine has learned a few things during our marriage. You won't want to leave this conflict unresolved through the night, but allowing her some time to process the situation is good. Better she argue with herself than you." She winked. "But each woman is unique as to how she handles being troubled. As your relationship grows and matures, you'll both figure out the best way to handle your differences. But it sounds as if you've done nothing wrong, and that your gift may have uncovered a disturbing memory."

Shoving his fists into his pockets, Flynn grimaced. "But why would she run away rather than tell me about it."

"Because you two barely know each other." She squeezed his arm. "If she's like I was when I met Alonzo, she's unsure if she can trust you with her heart yet." Flynn opened his mouth to respond, and she held up her hand. "Especially if it's been broken by someone in the past. You need to tread gently. You can't force a flower to bloom; you have to wait for the petals to unfurl after they've been exposed to water and light."

"She's right, Flynn." Alonzo pursed his lips. "You can't march in with those big feet of yours and ask what's wrong with her. That will make her feel she's to blame. Go in with an apology for distressing her. She may or may not share what's bothering her, but it will ease the burden she's carrying."

Flynn tapped his chin. "I couldn't ask for two better friends. Thank you for your wise counsel. I've been at a loss, and this is one more unsettling incident."

Alonzo's eyebrow shot up. "How so?"

"Our period of correspondence was short, but there is a certain...cadence to her letters, her phrasing that is missing. And there have been a couple of occasions she claims to have forgotten what we talked about. How is that possible?"

Yvonne paled. "Are you saying she may not be Miss Dalton?"

"Not yet, but something is amiss. Her letters were full of her love of God and how she couldn't wait to serve Him together. This woman rarely speaks of the Lord, initially seemed hesitant to attend church, and even now seems to only go through the motions."

"That's a serious allegation, Flynn." Alonzo narrowed his eyes. "She's lived here less than a month. Not a long time to feel comfortable. Think about when you first arrived. Were you as confident as you are now?"

"No, you make a valid point." He forked his fingers through his hair. "Maybe I'm overreacting, and her behaviors can be explained away."

"Have you prayed about this?" Yvonne's voice was soft.

His face warmed. "Not as much as I should."

"I've said enough, Flynn, and I'll be praying for you both." She winked. "But now I'm going to find our girl and see what I can do to patch things up between you."

"I thought you said—"

"You will need to apologize, but sometimes a mediator is in order." She wagged her finger at Flynn, then kissed Alonzo's cheek. "Don't wait for me. I'll make my own way home." She lifted her skirts and hurried out the door.

Alonzo crossed his arms and looked smug. "I don't know what I did to deserve that woman, but I'm glad she agreed to marry me."

Flynn snorted a laugh, then sobered. "She is a blessing. I don't know what I'd do without you two." He paced to the window and looked outside. "Am I seeing artifice where there is none? The matrimonial agency is a reputable firm, and Mrs. Crenshaw is a woman of integrity who performs background checks on her clients. Surely, she would have unearthed a nefarious past if Miss Dalton...this woman...has one."

"All true, but you're an intelligent man, and if your gut is telling you something is askew, you should follow your instincts." He leveled his gaze at Flynn. "What are you going to do if your bride-to-be isn't Miss Dalton?"

"I don't know." Flynn's stomach clenched. "But if this isn't Jessica, where is she, and why didn't she come?"

"Perhaps she couldn't." Alonzo shook his head. "And perhaps this woman had something to do with why."

Chapter Thirteen

A soft knock sounded at the door to her room, and Rayne swiped at the tears on her face. She grimaced at the mirror that reflected her blotchy face, red nose, and puffy, red-rimmed eyes. Jessica managed to look ethereal when she sobbed. Not Rayne. There was no adjective for how awful she looked after crying.

The rapping sounded again. "Miss Dalton? Jessica?" Yvonne's voice was muffled. "May I come in?"

What was she doing here? "Just a moment." Rayne swallowed the lump in her throat, then grabbed her hankie and dried her face. She smoothed her skirts, pulled the pins from her hair, brushed her tangled locks, then plaited it in a long braid. Her face was still a mess, but she couldn't stall any longer. She padded across the room and opened the door. "Yes?"

"I came to see how you are faring. May I visit with you?"

"Uh, okay." Why did everyone have to be so nice? Their behaviors would make it that much harder to leave. She stepped back and gestured for the young woman to enter.

Yvonne squeezed Rayne's arm as she slipped past. Her gaze roamed the room, and a smile curved her lips. "Are you comfortable here?"

Rayne shrugged. "While not spacious, the accommodations are lovely. Certainly much nicer than anywhere I've lived." She pointed to the chair in the corner as she sank onto the bed. "Please make yourself at home."

"Thank you for seeing me." Yvonne sat and crossed her ankles, then laced her fingers. "We don't know each other well, but I'm here to help if I can. I don't want to pry into your business or Flynn's, but I thought having a woman to talk with might make you feel better."

"I appreciate your kindness." Rayne hunched her shoulders. "Everyone has been friendly...accepting, yet they barely know me. I don't understand."

"Have you ever lived in a small town?"

"No. I was born and raised in Portland. The city is all I know."

"In a community our size, we rely on each other, but not just for physical needs. Rocky Mountain Springs is remote and can be a lonely place, so we draw close to each other."

"Our apartment was one of hundreds in a broken-down building. We went to work before dawn and came home after dinner. We ate and slept at home, nothing more. No socializing."

Yvonne frowned. "How sad for you. What a difficult way to live." She brightened. "You gave up everything to come to Wyoming. We want you to love it here as much as we do."

"I'm trying." Rayne tugged at her cuffs. "The change has been more overwhelming than I anticipated. Nothing is the same for me, and the feeling is a bit disconcerting."

"I've walked in your shoes and can attest to the fact that it will take time for you to feel at home. Flynn understands, which is why he didn't want to rush you into marriage, but at some point you will have to agree to wed. Please don't leave him waiting for too long." She tilted her head. "Have you changed your mind about the arrangement? Is that why his gift upset you? Do you not see yourself caring for him as a wife at some point?"

Rayne rose and walked to the window. She parted the curtains and stared down into the street. Wagons rattled through the dusty thoroughfare, and pedestrians hurried in and out of the merchants. Without turning, she said, "Flynn is a wonderful man. Sometimes too good to be true."

A snicker came from behind her, and Yvonne said, "Trust me, he's not."

Smiling, Rayne pivoted and went back to the bed. "I don't suppose you'd be willing to share some of his faults."

"I'll let you discover his shortcomings on your own." Yvonne tittered. "But he's a good man, a worthy man, more to the point, a godly man. One who will cherish you and treat you as you deserve."

"But don't you see, I don't deserve his care. I didn't do anything to earn it. I simply showed up."

"You don't give yourself enough credit. First of all, coming here is a big deal. As I said, you've left all that is familiar. But secondly, you've jumped into the mercantile with both feet. I've never seen more attractive displays. You've got a talent for arranging the products. And third, you make Flynn happy. He hasn't smiled this much since I've known him." She narrowed her eyes. "But perhaps there's something you're not telling me. I don't want to see Flynn hurt. Is the real reason for your reaction to the gift going to hurt him?"

Her shoulders sagged, and Rayne's gaze shot to Yvonne's wary expression. "I don't know. Perhaps. At a minimum, he'll be disappointed." She pressed a hand against her stomach that buzzed as if a swarm of bumblebees had taken flight. "I'm not a believer."

Yvonne nodded as if Rayne's declaration came as no surprise.

"I...uh...know about God, and I attended church in Portland with my sister, but she's the one who accepted Jesus, not me." She licked her lips. "You don't seem shocked."

"I'm not." Yvonne's eyes sparkled. "Think about how your sister and others in your church acted. There are certain behaviors and phrases often prevalent among believers that you don't exhibit. Coupled with your initial reluctance to attend services made me wonder about the veracity of the claims in your letters."

Rayne's mouth twisted. "Does Flynn share your opinion?"

"No, although he senses there is something awry." Yvonne reached for Rayne's hand. "Do you want to become a believer? Do you feel God's pull on your heart?"

"He would never accept me. I'm not good enough. I've done too many things."

"Jessica, no sins are too big for God to forgive. He wants you in His family. We humans have trouble forgiving ourselves, but He does not."

Pulse skipping, Rayne trembled. God would expect her to confess everything to these people. She knew that much from things her sister had said. It was bad enough Rayne hadn't been able to convince them about being a believer, but she couldn't admit to being an imposter. Not yet. Maybe not ever. "I-I'm not ready."

"I understand, but you will need to discuss this with Flynn. He has a right to know."

"But do we have to tell him right away? Can't we keep this conversation to ourselves for a bit? While I figure things out?"

Yvonne crossed her arms and studied Rayne for a long moment. She gave her a curt nod. "I'm not comfortable with this, but I'm willing to give you a couple of weeks. If you don't say anything by the summer solstice, I will."

"Thank you." Rayne dropped her gaze.

"Our faith doesn't allow us to be paired with nonbelievers, and a relationship built on deception is not healthy." She rose and hugged Rayne. "I like you. A lot. And I think you could be the perfect fit for Flynn." She patted Rayne's shoulder. "I'll let myself out."

The door closed, and Yvonne's words hung in the air. Rayne flopped facedown on the bed and put the pillow over her head. If possible, the situation was worse than before.

Chapter Fourteen

From behind the counter, Flynn peeked across the mercantile at Miss Dalton bent over a display. A slight sheen of perspiration covered her cheeks, and her frazzled hair created a halo around her face. She straightened and studied the shelves while tapping a finger on her chin. Sunlight through the window glistened on her hair, capturing the red and gold highlights. He swallowed and looked back at the ledger before she detected his stare.

The numbers on the page swam, and he rubbed his eyes. Normally, he loved tallying the figures of the business, but he could barely concentrate today. Two days had passed since he'd given Miss Dalton the drawing paper and pencils. Yvonne had returned from speaking to her with the news that his intended agreed to discuss what was bothering her no later than the summer solstice. A fortnight.

In the meantime, they each focused on their responsibilities in the shop and stuck to topics like the weather and local news when they sat down for meals. Shadows lurked in her eyes, and she never quite met his gaze. What sort of information would make her so wary?

He'd pressed Yvonne after her conversation with Miss Dalton, but she refused to reveal what they'd discussed, indicating it was not her news to share. She assured him she was praying for the two of them, and she felt the situation could be resolved. She'd also claimed she had no plans to let Alonzo in on their exchange, so he couldn't finagle the information from his best friend, who was notorious for his inability to keep secrets.

Closing the journal, Flynn laid down the pencil, then grabbed the order book. He perched on the stool and reviewed the purchase requests. The bell on the door tinkled, and the Delaney sisters tottered into the shop. He lifted his hand in greeting. "Hello, ladies. May I help you?"

Ethel shook her head. "We're here to see Miss Dalton. She makes the most wonderful recommendations on fabrics, pairing colors we never would have considered. She has quite the eye for style, don't you know."

"Very good." He gestured toward the back of the store. "She's working on a new display."

Emmie clapped her hands, and Ethel's eyes glowed. "Excellent! We can't wait to see what she's done. I hope you realize what a treasure she is."

His face warmed. "Yes I do."

They wended their way through the shelves and stacks of feed, chattering between themselves. Miss Dalton looked up as they approached, her face wreathed in smiles, her eyes clear.

Flynn sighed. Apparently she was guarded only around him. What was her news?

The Delaney sisters giggled like schoolgirls, something he'd never heard them do until Miss Dalton's arrival. Ethel was right, his intended was a treasure. She'd taken to the work in the mercantile as if born to it. Her eye for displays and merchandising was creative, combining items he'd never considered selling together. In addition, she cleaned the shop top to bottom on a regular basis to ensure the products were dust free, a chore he'd been haphazard about at best. Her head for numbers rivaled his own, and he could depend on her to proof his work quickly and accurately.

All the qualities of a good employee. Not a wife.

Maybe he shouldn't expect them to fall in love with each other. She had her secrets. He had a few of his own. Maybe they were only destined for friendship and affection. Was that enough for a successful marriage? Should he be willing to accept that they might not share the passion, joy, and devotion he saw in his friends' relationship? No, he'd rather get a dog for companionship than exist in a loveless marriage.

He completed the order form, wrote the check, then stuffed the items into an envelope. A walk to the post office might clear his head. At a minimum, leaving would keep him from staring at Miss Dalton like a moonstruck calf. Grabbing his hat from the hook, he called out, "Would you mind the store? I've got an errand to run."

She glanced toward him, the cautious look he'd come to expect back in her eyes. "Okay. Will you be gone long?"

"Not terribly. Do you need something?"

"No, just wondering."

The Delaney sisters seem to watch their exchange like a lawn tennis game, their necks swiveling back and forth.

"Have a nice day, ladies." Flynn yanked open the door and marched outside. He strode through the crowds and moments later arrived at his destination. Slipping inside he queued up and waited. His gaze wandered to the board nailed to the wall next to the clerk's window. Several Most Wanted posters were tacked to the board, some of which featured the distinctive logo of the Pinkerton Detective Agency. The all-seeing eye on the paper stared back at him above the proclamation "We Never Sleep."

Was a private detective the answer? Should he contact the Pinkertons and ask them to conduct a background check on Miss Dalton? Would they unearth something Mrs. Crenshaw had not? She'd used the Pinkertons, but like any industry, some employees were more skilled than others. Or should he bide his time and wait until the solstice deadline?

One by one, the people in front of him were served and left the building until his turn arrived. He laid the letter and some coins on the sill.

"What do you know about the Pinkertons, Eli? Are there any agents in Wyoming?"

The man slapped a stamp on the envelope and shrugged. "Probably in Cheyenne and some of the big towns. Why, you got a problem?"

"Perhaps, but it's too early to know."

"Their main office is in Chicago. I would imagine you could send a telegram, and they'd set you straight."

"Thanks. I might do that." Flynn touched the brim of his hat and pivoted, skirting a woman and three children. He left the building and hurried back to the mercantile, his mind racing. Inside, Miss Dalton stood behind the counter ringing up Mr. Bucknell's housekeeper. The Delaney sisters were nowhere to be seen.

Flynn hung up his hat. "Everything go okay?"

"Yes, why wouldn't it?" Her eyebrow lifted.

"Uh, no reason." He marched to the storeroom and stopped in front of the garden display. Eye-catching and clever, the presentation showcased a variety of tools, seeds, and other supplies. He took a small watering can from a nearby shelf, shifted the bucket of tools on the shelf to make room, then set down the container.

"I thought the displays were my responsibility."

Flynn startled.

Miss Dalton stood behind him, hands on her hips and her mouth set in a slash. "If you didn't like what I'd done, you should have told me."

"No, that's not it." He removed the can from the shelf and put the other items back in place. "You've done a lovely job. I...uh...noticed there was no watering can and thought it would make a nice addition. But I should have left it alone."

"You're not just saying that, are you? I know our interaction has been awkward, but to take away my duties because we're floundering seems unreasonable."

"I'm doing nothing of the sort. Please, accept my apologies." He bowed. "I'll be in the back should you need me." He turned on his heel and stalked to the storeroom. Why had he thought a mail-order bride was a good idea?

Chapter Fifteen

A knock resonated at the door, and Rayne's heart jumped. Who would come visit her at the hotel at this hour of the morning? She laid the brush on the dresser and padded across the room. She opened the door, and her jaw dropped. "Flynn...I mean, Mr. Wade. Is there something wrong? Is it later than I think?"

He flushed to the roots of his hair as he shook his head. "Nothing wrong, and I'm sorry if it's too early. I'm sorry for our set-to last night. I should never interfered with your display. My doing so gave you the wrong idea. Even after years in this country, I sometimes forget that American women are independent creatures with strong opinions. I also realized we're not getting acquainted so much as simply working side by side. I'd like to remedy the situation, so I made arrangements for Liam from church to work the mercantile today. The lad sometimes covers for me when I've got pressing business. I'd like us to take the day off. Together. I thought we'd start with breakfast downstairs, and then go horseback riding. You've not seen much of the area, so we can do a bit of a tour—" A crooked grin lit his face, and his eyes twinkled. "And I'm rambling, aren't I?"

"Just a bit." She smiled, and her breath hitched. The whole day alone. Could she keep her wits about her?

"I hope you'll accept my apology and allow us to begin again." His eyes shifted, and uncertainty marred his expression.

She realized he was awaiting her answer, and she dipped her head. "You're forgiven. I've been oversensitive, letting my experiences at the cannery make me suspicious of your motives. I'd be pleased to spend the day with you, but I've only ridden a horse once. Perhaps a carriage ride instead?"

"If you're going to be a woman of the West, you'll need to learn to ride, and there's no time like the present." He winked. "I have every confidence you can do this. You've proven yourself to be a quick study."

"At least one of us is sure." Dampness sprang to her palms. Would she make a complete fool of herself, proving without a shadow of a doubt she was not the wife he needed? "Give me a few minutes, and I'll change into something more suitable, then meet you in the lobby."

He rubbed his hands together. "I'll make arrangements for a table in the restaurant. Take all the time you need." He bowed, then turned and strode down the hallway.

Rayne stifled the urge to watch him descend the stairs and closed the door. She'd never met a man like Flynn. His courtly manners made her feel ladylike and special. His polished accent was musical and sent thrills up her spine. He'd taken the blame for her overreaction, graciously claiming fault. She didn't deserve someone like him. The ride would give her the lay of the land, and she'd know which direction to flee when it was time.

Who was she kidding? It was past time to leave, but she couldn't bring herself to go. She'd lived in Portland since birth, but for some strange reason this tiny town in the mountains of Wyoming made her feel like she was finally home. As if she'd been running her whole life and now had a place of rest.

"Stop woolgathering, Rayne, and take one day at a time." She quickly stripped her work clothes and donned a plain cotton dress. Too bad she didn't have a split skirt, but this outfit would have to do. She wouldn't be here long enough to need a riding garment. Her stomach hollowed at the thought. She grabbed her reticule and hurried from the room.

She descended the stairs, and he held out his arm. She slid her hand into the crook of his elbow. The warmth of his shoulder permeated her sleeve, sending a jolt to her wrist.

Flynn led her into the dining room, where they had a quick, but filling breakfast. He regaled her with stories of his growing-up years in

England, putting on a brave face, but she sensed the bittersweet flavor of the memories.

The waitress approached carrying a small basket. "Sandwiches, fruit, and cookies, Mr. Wade. Probably more than you can eat, but the cook wanted to be sure you had enough. Leave the basket at the livery, and one of the dishwashers will retrieve it."

"Thank you." He laid money on the table. "Tell the cook breakfast was exceptional."

"He'll be pleased, sir." She set down the hamper. "Will there be anything else?"

"No, we'll be on our way." He held out his hand, and Rayne grasped his fingers. Her eyes widened at the warmth of his calloused skin against hers. How could his touch affect her so deeply after only three weeks in his presence?

They left the hotel and sauntered to the stables, the morning sun evaporating the dew that coated the grass. The earthy scent of dirt, manure, and animals greeted her as she and Flynn entered the massive barn. A man walked toward them leading two horses, and her pulse skittered. The animals seemed to loom over her, even at her height. She gaped at Flynn. "They're so...big."

"No larger than normal." He grinned. "Come, meet Blossom. She's the gentlest horse you'll ever know."

Rayne's heart thudded in her chest, and she inched forward. The mare nickered, then bobbed her head. Rayne held out her hand, and the horse snuffled her fingers.

"Good girl." Flynn squeezed her shoulder.

"Me or the horse?" She sent him a saucy smile.

He threw back his head and laughed, his eyes crinkling. "Which answer won't get me into trouble?"

She cocked her head and giggled. "I haven't decided."

Opening the saddlebags on the stallion, he tucked the towel-wrapped food into the compartments, then handled the basket to the groom. "The hotel will retrieve this later." He took the reins for Blossom and handed them to Rayne, then explained the various part of the tack and what to do to control the horse. "I hope it's okay that I had them give you a sidesaddle."

Bile rose in her throat, and breakfast threatened to reappear. She swallowed and nodded. How hard could this be?

"Ready?"

"As I'll ever be."

He chuckled and helped her climb into the saddle, his hands firm on her waist. The feel of his hands lingered as she watched him mount the horse in a practiced, fluid motion. His muscles strained against his jacket, and she blinked, her mouth going dry. Why did he have to be so handsome?

"After you, m'lady." He gestured for her to lead the way out of the stable.

She clicked her tongue and lifted the reins. Blossom stepped forward, and Rayne expelled a loud breath. She grinned and looked over her shoulder at Flynn. "I'm doing it."

"Well done." Flynn winked. "Or should I say good girl?"

"Ha. Very clever." She loosened her grip on the leather straps and forced the tension from her shoulders. Was it true animals could smell fear? If so, Blossom would know she was terrified, but she refused to let Flynn know.

The morning passed quickly as they explored the town and outlying areas. Nothing like the cramped streets of Portland, the rugged landscape was beautiful. Birds swooped overhead in the cloudless sky. The distant mountains were snowcapped even in early June. Rayne became comfortable in the saddle, and she periodically patted Blossom's neck in appreciation of the horse's placid nature.

They stopped next to a small stream and ate lunch, Rayne more hungry than she imagined possible. The horse had done all the work, while she merely rode on top.

Flynn folded the towels, then rose and stuffed them into the saddlebags. He ruffled his hair and squinted at the sun. "We should probably start back."

Rayne pushed herself to her feet, muscles quivering. She stumbled, then regained her balance. Her face flamed.

"We've overdone." He slapped his forehead. "Shame on me for keeping you on the trail so long. You're going to be hurting tomorrow, and it will be my fault."

"It's okay. I had to get broken in sooner or later."

"But not all in one day." With his hand in the small of her back, he led her to the horse, then lifted her into the saddle. "I've—"

"Don't move!" Rayne shrieked.

Three feet in front of her horse, a snake raised its head and hissed. The eerie sound of rattling filled the air.

Flynn yanked out his pistol and fired. The snake collapsed in a heap.

Startled by the shot, Blossom reared. The reins pulled from Rayne's hands, and she grabbed for the saddle horn. Her moist palms couldn't find purchase. She tumbled to the ground, her shoulder hitting the hard-packed earth.

He rushed to her side and knelt on the ground. "Jessica! Are you okay?" He ran his fingers over her arms, then her legs. "Praise God, nothing seems to be broken."

She groaned. Every inch of her body hurt, but what pained her most was Flynn's use of her sister's name. He seemed to care for her, but he still thought she was Jessica, the Bible-believing Christian who'd written him. "I'm fine. Just bruised, but God had nothing to do it. He doesn't know me. Why would He care enough to keep me from breaking my neck?"

"What?" Flynn reared back as if she'd slapped him. "I don't understand."

"I'm not a believer, Flynn." Her lips trembled. "My sister was, but not me. God will never let me in. I'm not good enough." She dropped her gaze and inspected her palms, scuffed and stinging, just like her heart.

Chapter Sixteen

His heart thundering in his chest, Flynn stared at Miss Dalton. This couldn't be happening. In the span of a breath, his life turned upside down. He'd been wary about securing a bride through an agency, and this women's deceit confirmed that he should have gone with his gut and passed on the idea.

She'd sounded genuine in her letters. Her knowledge of the Bible seemed extensive, and the faith woven throughout the correspondence authentic. Had she not written the words? Did she get help from a friend, the two of them reading his missives and determining how to answer so he would choose her.

A chill swept over him. Was this a prank to see if she could get a man to fall in love with her, then walk away having succeeded...his scalp on her belt. Were there others she'd hoodwinked? What type of woman pretends to be something she's not? He'd prayed over the replies he'd received and felt God leading him to select her. Had he misread his Lord's prompting? Or did He have a plan in this mess?

"Why?" Flynn's voice caught. "Why would you pretend?" Did he want to know the answer? She at least had the decency to look ashamed, but that didn't excuse her actions.

Her mouth worked, but no words came out. Tears tumbled down her cheeks, and she wrapped her arms around her middle.

He shifted and sat on the ground, then laced his fingers and waited. Waited for her to bring order to his world. To tell him this was an elaborate joke and she was teasing him. But from her flushed face, lifeless eyes, and quivering chin, he knew the truth. This was no laughing matter.

She continued to remain mute, her shoulders heaving with her sobs. His throat thickened, and he swallowed against the lump that had formed. How could he be so angry, yet touched by her tears? He pulled out his handkerchief and dropped it in her lap. He dare not touch her in case the familiar tingles he felt would betray him.

Minutes crawled, and her cries lessened. She mopped her face with the linen and took a shuddering breath. Dampness clung to her lashes. "I'm sorry." Her voice was barely above a whisper. "I'm so sorry for lying. I was so miserable, and coming here seemed like the answer. Then I arrived and hoped I could fumble my way clear. I wanted to tell you. I did, but..." She lifted one shoulder in a tired shrug.

"I must know. Did you write the letters? How did you sound so...perfect?"

"No, my sister. She's the believer."

"Oh." His stomach hollowed. *Dear God, what would You have me do?* He'd come to care for her, but a marriage was out of the question. There was a reason the Bible prohibited Christians from being unequally yoked with nonbelievers. A marriage that merged two people with opposing worldviews couldn't succeed. He scrubbed at his face with cold fingers. What now?

He'd grown to care for her. With her intelligence, wit, tenacity, and gentleness, she'd burrowed her way into his heart. No other woman affected him as she did, yet he'd have to turn her away.

Unless she came to faith. Was she close? Should he marry her knowing she might eventually come to the Lord? A tricky proposition at best.

Flynn scooted near her and tucked a loose strand of silky hair behind her ear. "Do you want to believe?"

"I don't know. Yvonne asked me the same question." She licked her lips. "I've been reading J—my sister's Bible, and listening to Pastor Taggart's sermons. But I don't think God wants me. He's been punishing me most of my life...my father couldn't keep a job, so we were raised in poverty, then our parents died and we lost our home. Finally, we found the cannery and a place to live, but it was so awful." Tears flowed again. "Then she died."

"Who?" He took her hand in his and stroked the back with his thumb. "Who died?"

"My sister. She got hurt at work, and the doctors couldn't save her." She sighed. "Why didn't God save her?" She lifted pain-filled eyes to Flynn. "Now I'm alone."

"I'm sorry about your sister. That must have been difficult." He squeezed her fingers. "But you have me. And Yvonne and Alonzo."

"Don't you hate me?" She extricated her hand from his. "You must."

"I admit you've hurt me with this revelation, and I'm angry at being conned. My emotions are all tangled up, but I don't hate you." He stroked her jaw with his index finger. "I could never hate you. However, to be honest, this changes things. I don't know if we should wed."

"I understand. I'll pack my things and leave before I do any more damage."

"No."

Her gaze shot to his face. "You don't want me to go?"

"You've got no one in Portland, and you need the support of friends. I'd like to be your friend." *Please God, let this work out so we can be more than friends.* "I know Yvonne and Alonzo will want you to remain here, too."

Skepticism darkened her eyes. "How can you speak for them?"

"Because I know they care for you as much as I do." He rose and held out his hand. "Please say you'll stay. We'll figure things out later, but for today, please agree to wait to make your decision about leaving."

She studied his face for a long moment, then nodded. "It's a deal." She grasped his fingers and pulled herself to her feet, then tucked her hands into her pockets. "And Flynn, I truly am sorry for hurting you. That wasn't my intention."

He gestured to the horses, and they made their way to the animals who stood patiently grazing under a copse of trees. He stepped over the morass of roots and turned to guide her across the protruding branches, but her heel caught, and she stumbled. Her hands splayed across his chest as she looked up at him, her eyes wide. Her breath tickled his cheek. "How foolish of me."

"It could happen to anyone." He continued to hold her, and before he could change his mind, he lowered his head and pressed his mouth to hers. Her lips softened under his, and her arms twined around his waist. He deepened the kiss. He'd think about the ramifications later. Much later.

Chapter Seventeen

The whiskers of Flynn's beard and moustache tickled her skin, and Rayne's toes curled, her arms tightening around Flynn. His lips were warm and firm, yet gentle. Her pulse raced. Blossom shifted and nudged her shoulder, breaking her kiss with Flynn. Still inches from his, her face heated. Good girls don't give themselves over to passionate kisses, even nonbelievers.

She slipped from his embrace and turned toward the horse, fiddling with the girth on the saddle. "We should get back, don't you think?"

A pause, then he cleared his throat. "Sure, although we can continue to tour if you'd like. There is still plenty to see."

Tugging at the leather strap, she nodded. He was going to grant her the favor of pretending the kiss didn't happen. A true gentlemen. Which was one of the things she loved about him. Because she did love him.

Somewhere during the weeks of working side by side at the mercantile, sitting together on the hard pews at church and talking with him during meals, she grown to love him. And not simply for his handsome looks. His integrity in business, spending hours bent over the books to determine fair prices for his customers that would allow him to earn a living was like nothing she'd ever seen, certainly not at the cannery. He was intelligent, his mind sharp and quick. Kind to a fault, he treated her like a true partner, seeking her opinion and valuing her contributions to the store no matter how small.

She nibbled the inside of her cheek, then smiled. Flynn also made her laugh, his sense of humor dry and clever. He'd wear a deadpan expression when telling a joke, his eyes twinkling in delight. But the trait that drew her most was his love of God. Even though she was not a believer, his steadfast trust that God loved all people, and his faith that the Lord was in control pulled at her heart, provoking unfamiliar feelings. She wanted the peace Flynn had, and according to him, he need only pray and ask for it.

Her chest tight, she checked the reins, then patted Blossom's muzzle. Not yet. She wasn't ready to accept that God really wanted her. And she wouldn't commit just so she could marry Flynn.

She climbed into the saddle and peeked at Flynn, who waited astride his stallion. He smiled at her as if nothing had happened between them. Again, being a gentleman. She pinned on a smile and clicked her tongue. Blossom moved forward, and Flynn guided his horse to her side.

As they rode, he named the peaks that surrounded them. He pointed to a herd of animals grazing at the edge of the forest. "Those are antelope, pronghorn to be specific. Their coloring is distinctive. Do you see the white fur on their rumps, bellies, and throats?"

"Beautiful." Rayne squinted at the graceful animals. "Some are much smaller. Are those the babies?"

He grinned. "Yes, and they're called fawns. I guess you don't see too much wildlife in Portland."

"Not hardly." A giggle erupted from her. "They're magnificent."

"They're one of my favorite animals here. Amazing to watch them run. I read somewhere pronghorn are the fastest mammal on the continent."

"Even horses?" She cocked her head and watched the antelope saunter, heads down, munching on the uneven grass covering the meadow.

"So I've been told." His face lit, and he snapped his fingers. "There's one more place I'd like to show you before we return to town."

"What is it?"

"A surprise, but not far from here." He winked and kneed his stallion, and the animal began to trot.

Blossom picked up her pace, and Rayne gripped the reins, her scraped palms protesting. One tumble was sufficient, but his eagerness spurred her on. He led her into the woods, and they picked their way through the underbrush. Minutes later, she heard a deafening roar, louder that any noise the cannery made. The trees cleared. A cascading waterfall surged over granite rocks into a river where it churned and foamed.

She gaped at Flynn as the sound reverberated and thundered in her chest.

"Speechless, aren't you?" His eyes shone. "I can't believe I almost forgot to bring you here. This is one of my favorite places to come, especially when I'm overwhelmed by life. The majesty of it all reminds me that God is bigger than my problems."

Rayne blinked back tears. But would a God who created this wondrous sight want someone so flawed as her? "It's beautiful. Thank you for showing me." She slid from the saddle and walked to the edge of the river, her gaze drinking in the verdant woods, smelling of moist earth. Squirrels cavorted in the branches, their chattering muffled by the rumble of the falls. A carpet of fallen leaves from years of past autumns cushioned her steps.

"Do you feel how the temperature has dropped? I don't understand the science of it, but no matter how hot it is in the valley, this area is significantly cooler. And despite this hardly being still waters, I'm reminded of the twenty-third psalm."

"Somehow restful even through its power."

"Exactly."

She stuffed her hands into the pockets of her dress, staring at the scene. Behind her, Flynn murmured to the horses, then fell silent. She'd been mesmerized the first time she'd seen Jewell Falls in Portland, but the puny Maine waterfall was nothing in comparison to this imposing torrent.

Something tickled her cheek, and she squealed, swiping at her face and flailing her arms. "What—"

Flynn chuckled and waved a feathery branch covered in short needles. He wore a broad grin.

She shuddered and slapped his arm. "Shame on you."

"I couldn't help myself."

A giggle escaped, then she sobered. "We can't do this."

"Do what?"

"Take our relationship any further. I don't have your faith, and I won't ask your God to accept me under false pretenses just so we can marry. I'm sorry." She climbed on the horse and flicked the reins. "Hyah."

Blossom trotted toward home, and Rayne pressed her lips together, willing herself not to give in to the sobs that threatened to overcome her. Her chest tightened, and the shards of her shattered heart created pain like she'd never experienced. Was it time to finally tell Flynn who she was or would that make the situation even worse?

Chapter Eighteen

Following Miss Dalton into the livery, Flynn slowed his stallion, then brought the animal to a stop. A pair of grooms hurried toward them to take the reins, and Flynn slid to the ground. He gave her space as she thanked the lads, then rushed from the barn. He pressed coins into their hands, then trailed her. Her statuesque form was easy to spot as she walked with purpose, looking neither left nor right, threading her way through the late afternoon crowd.

Still reeling from her revelation, he huffed out a deep breath. *Lord, I'm not sure what to do here. Why would You let this happen to me? Did I misread Your leading?*

He caught up with her at the entrance to the hotel and looped his arm with hers. She tried to pull away, but he held fast. "We need to finish this discussion." They entered the lobby, and he gestured to a trio of chairs nestled by one of the windows in the large room. "This should give us some privacy, unless you'd like to head to the mercantile."

"This is fine." Her jaw clenched, and she shook her head. "But there's nothing to discuss. Your biblical mandate says that we can't marry unless I accept Jesus as my Savior, and I can't do that. God doesn't want me. I've done too many bad things." She raised her gaze to his, her eyes filled with tears. "And if you knew everything about me, you'd reject me, too."

"Please sit." He pitched his voice low, gentle, as he might with a skittish horse. He didn't want her to bolt upstairs. "I'd like a chance to tell you my thoughts and feelings. Will that be all right with you?"

She studied him for a long moment, then nodded and dropped into one of the overstuffed chairs. She laced her fingers and lowered her gaze.

He leaned forward, his elbows propped on his thighs. Conversations punctuated with laughter swirled around them. His pulse skittered. How could he convince her of her value without putting her on the spot with a declaration of love?

Moisture sprang to his palms. Because despite his anger at being duped, he did love her. Mere weeks ago he couldn't imagine having a wife, and now he couldn't fathom his life without this woman. She completed him in a way no other person in his life did. They were two sides of the same coin. But if he told her of his love, and she didn't reciprocate his feelings...no, he wouldn't explore that possibility. She'd responded to his kiss...twice. Surely, she felt something for him.

"Yes, I'm upset...hurt at your dishonesty, and I only know what you chose to tell me in your letters, but it is enough for me to know that you were in dire straits. And in your desperation, you made the only decision you thought possible. Was it wrong? Yes. Unforgivable? No." He cleared his throat. "I've done things I'm not proud of, but God has forgiven me, and I try to follow His leading in everything I do. I still make a proper mess of my life if I'm not careful, but He knows I'm trying my best. That's all He expects of us."

She remained silent, her shoulders slumped.

"You said you wouldn't ask God to accept you under false pretenses so we could marry. That shows the kind of woman you are— filled with integrity and principles. I sense your uncertainty. You feel God's pull on your heart, but you're hesitant to set aside your past, to shed the burdens that weigh you down. I'd like to make a proposal to you."

Her eyes widened. "I can't—"

He held up his hand. "I'm sorry. A poor choice of words, but proposition seems even worse." One corner of her mouth curved, and the tension in his gut eased. "Let's take the wedding off the table. We're two friends. Friends who share many of the same interests, save one: God. I think if you got to know Him, you'd want Him in your life. Can you do me a favor and explore the possibility that God does love you, and nothing you've done changes that fact? You've listened to some sermons and heard me prattle on about Jesus, but have you done any studying on your own? Dug into the Bible to see what God is saying to you personally?"

"No. I tried, but..."

"Can be a bit overwhelming, can't it?"

She nodded.

"My favorite book is Luke. He was a doctor and wrote the book to a friend to instruct him about the reliability of the faith. Luke spoke with eyewitnesses and did a significant amount of research before writing his book, a letter really. Take your time and begin there. Then we can discuss it, and I can try to answer your questions. How does that sound?"

Her lower lip trembled, and his heart fell. To see her looking distraught was difficult, but he'd seen many people come to the Lord because they were so downtrodden the only option was to look up. He laid his handkerchief in her lap.

She wiped her eyes, then clasped the linen. "Thank you for being so gracious. I don't deserve your kindness."

"What kind of believer would I be if I rejected you for making a mistake? Especially in light of my own."

"I'll do what you ask. I promise."

"Flynn! Miss Dalton! There you are."

Flynn's head whipped toward the voice. He rose and shielded her from Alonzo and Yvonne, who rushed across the plush carpet toward them. "We took the day off and went riding. Is something wrong?"

Alonzo held up a basket, and Yvonne extended a towel-wrapped bundle. "I've done quite a bit of baking and brought you a loaf of bread and a cake." She grinned. "Shame on me for assuming you'd be at the mercantile. We stopped by, and Liam told us you were gone for the day."

"How lovely." He forced a smile and reached for the items. He tucked the bread under his arm and grasped the basket in the other hand. He glanced over his shoulder at Jessica's wan face. "I'm afraid I overexerted Miss Dalton. She's feeling under the weather."

Yvonne frowned and pushed past Flynn. "You poor dear. Let me help you to your room."

"Thank you, but I can—"

"Nonsense. You can't be expected to climb the stairs and get yourself into bed." She held out her arm. "Just loop your arm with mine, and we'll get you settled. And perhaps next time, Flynn won't bring you home in such a state."

"It's not his fault."

"I doubt it, but we'll leave that discussion for another time."

Flynn watched as they made their way across the lobby and up the stairs.

"This appears to be more than fatigue, my friend." Alonzo nudged his shoulder. "Care to talk?"

"You read me well." Flynn set the bread and cake on a small table, then gestured at the chairs he and Jessica had vacated. After they seated themselves, he outlined what happened, then sagged against the chair and blew out a loud breath. "Why would God allow this to happen?"

"I don't know, but He must have some plan we're not privy to." Alonzo leaned forward. "This is unbelievable. I don't understand how this would have gotten past Mrs. Crenshaw. She interviews her brides and grooms extensively."

"But somehow she was fooled as well."

Alonzo squeezed Flynn's knee. "You said Miss Dalton seems open to seeking God. I'll pray she finds Him."

Flynn rubbed the back of his neck. "Seems is the word. She also seemed to be someone she's not. Is she still fiddling with me? I told her we'd set aside the plan to marry and just be friends for now, but..."

"Your feelings run too deep."

"Yes." He grimaced. "Perhaps a better plan would be to break things off completely and send her away."

Chapter Nineteen

Standing behind the counter in the mercantile, Rayne bagged Alonzo's purchases, then handed him his change. Today was the first day she'd seen Flynn's best friend since blurting out her confession three days ago. Her heart had jumped into her throat when he'd walked in, but instead of anger or chastisement, he'd been friendly and warm. In between telling her what he needed to purchase, he'd chatted about the ranch and the weather: a constant source of conversation among the locals.

Why was he being nice to her? Was he trying to lull her into a false sense of belonging before he struck with razor-sharp words aimed at hurting her as much as she'd surely hurt Flynn? Flynn, who'd also been gracious, albeit not as open as before. When he thought she wasn't looking, his shoulders slumped and his eyes clouded. She swallowed the lump in her throat and pinned on a smile. How could Jessica have thought

Rayne taking her place was a good idea? Granted, her sister assumed Rayne would come to Wyoming as Rayne.

"Have a nice day, Alonzo. Give my best to Yvonne."

"Will do. She'd have come herself, but the baby is teething and fretful. She didn't want to subject anyone to his fussiness."

"I'd be happy to stop by to give her a break if you think that would be helpful." Rayne rubbed at a scratch on the wooden counter. Yvonne hadn't been to the shop since the *incident,* and she missed her cheerful demeanor. Her friend would be able to tell her how to shed the heaviness that permeated her mood.

"I'll let her know. The constant crying is tiring, so I'm sure she'll appreciate seeing you." He picked up his bag, then squeezed her arm with his other hand. "We're praying for you and Flynn." Before she could reply, he strode to the door and left the mercantile.

Thuds and bangs came from behind the curtain in the storage room where Flynn was putting away stock that had arrived on the morning train. The shop had been busier than usual with customers coming and going all morning. She hadn't been able to sit since arriving at work, so her back ached, and the balls of her feet burned. She lifted one foot and then the other as she shifted in an attempt to get comfortable while she continued to help customers with their purchases.

Thirty minutes later, the shop was finally vacant, and she sank onto the stool with a sigh. Noise from the stockroom had ceased, and she looked up as Flynn appeared from behind the curtain carrying a stack of boxes. He wended his way through the shelves and displays to set his load on the counter. He smiled, but the gesture didn't quite reach his eyes.

Her mouth dried, and she hopped off her seat.

"The items we ordered for the Fourth of July celebrations arrived. I thought you could do something fun with them in the front window."

"Wonderful. I'd love to. Thanks for asking me."

He shrugged. "Displays are what you're good at."

"Listen—"

The bell over the door rang, and the Delaney sisters entered, their faces beaming.

Rayne clamped her mouth and forced a smile.

Flynn bowed. "Good morning, ladies. To what do we owe the pleasure of your visit?"

Ethel tittered. "So proper, Mr. Wade. You make us feel like princesses of the court."

Emmie guffawed, her laugh reminiscent of a mule Rayne had seen once on the streets of Portland pulling a milk wagon.

"You're two of my favorite customers. Why not make you feel special?"

"Go on, you. We're much too old to be flirting with." Ethel thwacked him with her fan, then winked. "But we certainly appreciate it. We'd like to make arrangements for some canning jars to be delivered to the house. It's a bit early, but we want to be ready when the currants and gooseberries come on."

"Very wise. How many would you like?"

"Is four dozen too many? We don't want to take more than our fair share."

"You're not. I've plenty in stock with more on the way." He gestured to Rayne. "Miss Dalton can take care of you."

Ethel grinned. "Yes, she's quite smart. And beautiful, too. Why haven't you set a date for the wedding? Most mail-order brides marry almost as soon as they arrive." She cocked her head and wagged her finger at Rayne. "Do you find Mr. Wade lacking? We think he's a perfect catch. Smart, funny, successful, and very good looking. Wouldn't you agree?"

Rayne's face heated. "Well—"

"Now, Miss Delaney, it's not fair to Miss Dalton putting her on the spot like that. We're getting acquainted and will marry when the time is right. And you'll be among the first to receive an invitation."

Emmie snorted another laugh. "Don't take too long. She's not without her own many virtues. Any number of single men here in town may think you're not interested and step up to court this lovely young lady."

His face pinked. "Then I'll set them straight. Thank you for your concern." He picked up the charge slip from the counter and handed it to Ethel. "I can have one of the lads deliver the jars on Wednesday. Will that be soon enough?"

"Changing the subject, are you?" Ethel smirked and tucked the receipt into her reticule. "Suit yourself, but you're already in love, so why wait?"

Rayne gasped, and her gaze shot to Flynn whose jaw hung slack and cheeks were now as red as the Independence Day bunting.

The sisters waved and tottered out of the shop.

"Yes...well, that was awkward." Flynn cleared his throat and finger-combed his hair. "Are you all right?"

Nodding, she busied herself with the boxes. "I'm sure they mean no harm."

"Probably not, but I'll never get used to this aspect of small-town living, where a man's business is rarely his own."

"They're just vocalizing what most folks are thinking."

"My point exactly." He frowned. "Anyway, I'm going to the post office for the mail. I shouldn't be long."

"Would you rather I went?"

"After being cooped up in the back, I'd like to get some air." After a long look, he strode to the door, grabbed his hat, and headed outside.

Rayne closed her eyes. She'd hurt him. Badly. Yet he continued to treat her politely, and twice he'd asked her about her Bible reading, his face lighting up when she'd indicated she was halfway through the book of Luke and enjoying it. More than that, the words were convicting her of her wrongdoing. She needed to tell Flynn her identity. She'd planned to do it first thing this morning, but then she'd overslept and barely made it to the mercantile before they opened at eight o'clock. The constant flow of customers had prevented any in-depth dialogue. When he returned, she'd tell him they needed to talk after closing tonight.

Tears pricked the backs of her eyes. She should have packed her things last night to be prepared for leaving. Because once she told him the truth, she'd lose him. He'd demand she leave town unless he dragged her to the sheriff to have her arrested for impersonating her sister. *Dear God, I've made a royal mess of things.*

She blinked. Since when did she pray?

Clutching the envelope and newspaper clipping in his hand, Flynn stalked to the mercantile. Nausea threatened to overwhelm him, and he swallowed against the breakfast that threatened to reappear. Unease had slithered up his spine when he saw the penciled scrawl across the face of the envelope, then he'd opened it to find an article from the *Portland Daily Press*, and his unease had turned to despair.

There was no return address, but a Cheyenne cancelation marked the front. Who could have sent the story? And why wait a month to do so?

He stormed into the shop, and his gaze shot to Miss Dalton...the woman he now knew to be Rayne, not Jessica, his intended bride. There were no customers, so he locked the door and turned the CLOSED sign.

Her eyes traveled to the article in his hand. Her face paled, and her hand flew to her throat.

Waving the offending article, he marched toward her, then slapped the newspaper onto the counter. "How could you do this? I don't know what's worse: lying about being a believer or stealing your sister's identity." He shoved his fingers through his hair and stared at her.

Her mouth worked, but no words came out.

"Can't figure out how to fabricate a story to talk your way out of this, Miss Dalton? *Rayne*. I knew something was off, but I chose to think it was just nerves or the difficulties of living somewhere new or that we didn't know each other well. Then you admitted to not being a Christian, and I figured that's what was wrong." He stabbed at the paper. "Then I received this from Mr. Biggs, from your old company, confirming my suspicions that you aren't the woman I corresponded with. Were you ever going to tell me, or did you plan to be Jessica for the rest of your life?"

Tears tumbled down her cheeks. Biggs had followed through with his threat, and Flynn now knew the truth before she could confess. "I was going to tell you. I decided last night that I would do it today, but then I was nearly late for work, and we've had nonstop customers. Please, believe me. I knew I would lose you, but I was going to confess tonight."

"Bah! Why should I believe you? You've done nothing but lie since you arrived. You're a fraud and untrustworthy. You're probably faking your interest in becoming a believer."

"No, I—"

"Leave."

"But—"

"I don't want to have to call the sheriff to get you out of here, but I will."

She bent and grabbed her reticule from under the counter. Sobbing, she rushed to the door and fumbled with the lock. Without turning, she said, "I'm sorry for hurting you. So sorry. I don't blame you for hating me." She yanked opened the door and rushed outside, the bell tinkling merrily.

Flynn scrubbed at his face with cold fingers, then propped his elbows on the wooden counter and put his head in his hands. There was no need to read the article again. He'd memorized the words. Jessica had died after a workplace accident. She left behind a twin sister, her parents having perished in a fire several years prior. Had they cooked up the scheme before Jessica succumbed to her injuries, or was the entire farce Rayne's idea? If she was as miserable as Jessica had attested in her letters, she'd probably thought coming west would solve her problems. But why not contact him with the news about her sister and offer to come in her place?

He crumpled the article and hurled it against the wall. The ball ricocheted and bounced off his forehead, then landed on the floor. He should have contacted the Pinkertons when the idea first came to him. Then he wouldn't be living this nightmare. He was a fool from the very beginning and had played into her hands.

Was everything a lie? She'd seemed to enjoy his company, and she'd responded to his kiss as if she cared. If marriage to him was her goal, why didn't she fake a conversion?

Images of her danced through his mind. Her golden-brown eyes sparkling when she laughed. The small crease that formed between her eyebrows when she was concentrating. Her silky brown hair shimmering in the sunlight. She was a beautiful woman, but she was more than her physical features. She was one of the most intelligent people he'd ever met, man or woman. Her quick wit kept him hopping, and her probing of an issue challenged him.

Even after he'd discovered her initial duplicity, he'd told Alonzo he loved her. But how did he feel now? He'd been drawn to Jessica in her letters, but had his loved bloomed after he met Rayne or when he thought she was her sister.

Dear God, how could You let this happen?

Chapter Twenty

Slumped in her chair, Rayne propped her elbows on the kitchen table and dropped her chin into her hand. The morning sun peeked through the window over the sink, casting a beam across the floor. Yvonne busied herself at the stove, humming a song Rayne didn't recognize. Two days had passed since the debacle at the store, and she was no closer to a decision on what to do.

While in town with Alonzo, Yvonne had found her wandering the sidewalks shortly after the incident. She listened to Rayne's tale of woe, then gave her a hug and insisted she return home with them. Both had been warm and friendly, settling her into the small guest room and providing meals and companionship. Whenever she asked why they were being nice after she'd hurt Flynn, they talked about their faith and how God expected them to treat her. Yvonne had loaned her a Bible that contained many underlined verses, and she'd pored over the pages well into the night.

During the day, she helped Yvonne with the copious tasks of running a ranch, making her realize how much she preferred working at the mercantile to performing household chores. The endless focus on food whether harvesting, canning, preparing, or planning was tedious at best, yet her friend juggled the job with little stress.

Yvonne set a plate of scrambled eggs, fried potatoes, a ham steak, and two biscuits in front of her. Her mouth watered at the aroma, and she dug into the meal. "I wish you wouldn't wait on me. I don't deserve your kindness."

"Stop." Yvonne sank into the chair next to her and laid her hand on Rayne's shoulder. "You continue to apologize. I know you're genuinely sorry about what happened. I also know you had your reasons. That doesn't make what you did right, but I do understand why you did it." She laced her fingers and took a deep breath. "Eat up and listen to what I have to say."

"But—"

"You'll get your chance, but I want you to hear me out. Okay?"

Rayne pressed her lips together and nodded.

"I've watched you these past two days, and you're miserable. God is beckoning to you, yet you can't bring yourself to accept His call. You've said before that you don't feel worthy of Him. Let me tell you something: none of us are. He doesn't want us because we deserve His grace, but rather because He loves us. All you have to do is say yes to His free gift, and you'll never be the same." She smiled, her beaming face having nothing to do with the sun streaming into the kitchen. "Life won't be perfect, and there will be consequences from your actions, but you'll have a peace that will carry you through anything that happens."

Setting down her fork, Rayne wiped her mouth with the napkin, then pushed away her plate. Her eyes welled, and she wrapped her arms around her middle. "I've watched you and Alonzo, and I want what you have, the calmness in your spirit. I'm still struggling to believe that God wants me, but I'm exhausted from trying to handle things on my own." She sent Yvonne a wry smile. "And as you can see, I've made a perfect mess of it, so I want to say yes to Him. Will you help me?"

Yvonne enveloped her in a hug. "Of course. Just tell Him exactly what you said to me."

"Is there a special way I should form my words?"

"No. Talk to Him as if He's sitting beside you, because He is."

Rayne swiped at the moisture on her face, then bowed her head and closed her eyes. "Uh...God, it's me, Rayne. I'm sorry for all the bad things I've done, especially for the lying about being Je-Jessica. I don't want to run away from You anymore. Please accept me as Your child, and help me make amends for all the wrong I've done." Warmth blanketed her shoulders like a quilt, and her eyes flew open. Her head shot up, and she gaped at Yvonne.

Tears streaming down her cheeks, Yvonne embraced her again. "Welcome to the family," she whispered. "I'm so happy for you."

"I don't understand how I can feel so different in a matter of seconds. My heart still aches, but the pain isn't as sharp, more like it's been wrapped in cotton."

"The peace that passes all understanding. I've experienced it many times." Yvonne's forehead wrinkled. "God has forgiven you, but at some point soon you need to talk to Flynn and apologize, telling him everything."

"Can I write him a letter?" Rayne rubbed at a scratch on the table. "That way I could collect my thoughts."

"You need to do it in person. Give him a chance to respond. I'll go with you if you wish."

"No. I need to be brave and do this on my own." Rayne smiled. "Well, God will be with me."

"Exactly. You're learning already!"

"Then I'll need to figure out what comes next. If I stay here in Rocky Mountain Springs, I'll need to get a job and find a place to live." She nibbled the inside of her cheek. "I'm sure Flynn won't want me in the shop, but I don't know what other skills I have besides working in a factory. I'd rather avoid that if I could."

"We'll pray about it when you return. Flynn might surprise you and let you stay on. After all, he's short staffed."

"He'd have to be pretty desperate to continue employing me. But even if he does, I don't know if I can be with him every day, just being coworkers. And then when he finds another bride..." Her lips trembled, and she shrugged. "That would hurt too much."

"Rayne, even when life looks its bleakest, God is in control. The Bible tells us that all things work together for good for those who love the Lord. And if Flynn chooses not to marry you, God will heal your heart, but I have a feeling He's not done with the two of you yet."

Flynn gritted his teeth as the bell on the door clanged for the dozenth time that morning. Customers had been in and out of the shop quizzing him about the rumors surrounding Miss Dalton. He'd refused to answer their questions, but his reticence to discuss the situation only served to make them more curious.

His gaze shot to the telegram on the counter from Mrs. Crenshaw. He'd sent a cable informing her of the circumstances with Miss Dalton—he would never think of her as Rayne—and the agency owner had responded that she was praying for a resolution, and he should trust in God's plans. What kind of answer was that? Wasn't the woman outraged at being duped? What exactly did she think God was going to do about the situation?

The sheriff had shown up first thing and offered to arrest Miss Dalton for identity theft but said the judge might dismiss the case because she hadn't married Flynn, obtaining benefits by fraudulent means.

He didn't want to see her jailed, just out of his life, so he'd told the sheriff he'd let him know about pressing charges. Had everything been a lie? Had she faked her apparent enjoyment at working in the mercantile or pretended to care for him when she kissed him with such ardor?

"Mr. Wade, how are you today?" The Delaney sisters approached, concern etched on their faces. Ethel patted his arm. "We were stunned to hear about your young lady. You must be quite distraught."

"I'd rather not discuss Miss Dalton. Is there something I can help you find in the shop?"

Emmie pursed her lips. "Yes, we need several items, but we'll come back if you're too upset to wait on us."

Swallowing a retort, he bent and pulled out his sales pad from under the counter. "I'd be happy to assist you. Are you doing some more canning or perhaps working on a new quilt? Some lovely fabrics arrived on yesterday's train."

Their faces lit up, and they spoke in unison. "New material?"

"Yes, several bolts." Relief coursed through him. Sewing notions were like catnip to the pair. "Would you like to see them?"

"Eventually." Ethel tapped her chin. "But we wanted to let you know we're praying for you. What that woman did to you was terrible...unforgivable, and she should be punished. You must seek justice."

"Her business is not mine to share, but she had her reasons for acting as she did. She was in a bind, feeling desperate." He cocked his head. "And until we've walk in her shoes, we shouldn't judge her too harshly."

Emmie's eyebrow shot up. "You must love her very much to forgive so easily." She elbowed Ethel. "Come, Sister, we've said all we can. Let's peruse the material. I've a hankering to make a wedding quilt. I have a feeling we're going to need one as a gift."

Flynn's jaw dropped as he watched them saunter to the back of the shop. No matter how long he'd known the Delaneys, they always managed to surprise him. Of course, he'd surprised himself when he'd cautioned them against judging her, as if he hadn't been doing that very thing. How did Emmie know how he felt about Rayne? He'd barely figured it out for himself. She'd hurt him terribly through her deception, but sometime during the morning of defending her to his customers, his outrage had fizzled, and he realized he still cared for her.

Alonzo had informed him that they'd taken her in. Should he saddle his horse and head to the ranch so he could tell her...what? That he forgave her? A bold move to make before she asked for absolution. She might be offended at his action, thinking him arrogant.

What would she think he if told her of his love? He huffed out a breath and tugged at his collar. Telling her was out of the question.

Because until she became a believer, they couldn't marry even if a miracle occurred and she loved him in return.

Emmie waved her arm. "Mr. Wade, we're ready."

He wended his wave through the shop to the fabric counter. "What can I get you ladies?"

She pointed to three bolts and gave him the measurement information, then glanced at her sister. "Making our choice was difficult. Miss Dalton was always so helpful because she has a wonderful eye for color. Don't you think? It's a shame to lose her skills in the shop. I don't suppose you'd ask her to come back to work."

With a gulp, he shook his head. "I'm afraid that's not possible." It would be hard enough to see her around town and at church. He'd never be able to remain aloof if she was in the shop every day.

Chapter Twenty-One

Rayne squinted against the sun's glare as she climbed out of the wagon. She smoothed her skirt with trembling hands and drew in a large breath. "I won't be long." She shot Yvonne a crooked smile. "Especially if he refuses to let me in."

"Would you like me to go inside with you?"

"No, I need to do this on my own, but I appreciate you keeping me company on the drive."

"I'll be praying."

"Thank you." Rayne pressed a hand against her heart. "God's the only One who can fix this mess." She patted her hair and stepped onto the sidewalk as Flynn appeared in the window and flipped the CLOSED sign. She lifted her hand to catch his attention.

His eyes widened, and his lips thinned. He shook his head.

She mouthed, "Please. I won't be long."

He turned away, his broad shoulders stiff.

Her stomach hollowed. She came all this way, and he refused to see her. Rayne glanced over her shoulder at Yvonne. "He said no."

"Since when do you take no for an answer?" Yvonne tilted her head. "Show a little gumption. Maybe he wants to know how serious you are about seeing him."

"Okay." Rayne straightened her spine and lifted her chin. She raised her hand and knocked on the window.

Flynn wheeled around, a deep frown on his face. "What do you want?" His voice was muffled, but his anger was evident.

"I'd like to speak with you. Please let me in."

He glared at her through the window, his gray eyes like flint. He crossed his arms and continued to stare.

Fine. She could be just as stubborn. "Flynn, I'm here to apologize as well as tell you something. I can do it out here at the top of my lungs so you can hear me through the door, or you can let me in so we can do this in private."

To her left a couple exiting the butcher shop gaped at her. Her face burned, but she nodded an acknowledgment and remained rooted in front of the mercantile. She looked back at Flynn. "Would you—"

He opened the door and yanked her inside, then dropped his hand as if scalded. "There's no reason to make a scene." He fiddled with the cuffs of his shirt. "Now, say what you're here to say, but be quick about it. I've got somewhere I need to be."

Heart thudding in her chest, she licked her lips that had suddenly gone dry. The scent of his aftershave tickled her nose, and she stuffed her fists into the pockets of her dress before she gave in to temptation and grabbed his hands. "Ah, yes, of course." She cleared her throat. He must think her a ninny. "Thank you for seeing me. I appreciate you taking—"

"Get on with it." The muscle in his jaw jumped.

Tears sprang to her eyes, and a lump formed in her throat. She swallowed with effort. "I'm sorry. I'm here to ask your forgiveness for the trouble I've caused and because of my deception. You didn't deserve that, and I'm truly sorry for hurting you."

"That's it?" Sparks seemed to shoot from his eyes. "You're sorry."

"Yes. What I did was stupid, and I hurt many people in the process, especially you. It was my idea, not Jessica's, to take her identity. When she realized she was dying she told me to come to Wyoming in her place, but that didn't mean she wanted me to be her. She was trying to take care of me." Rayne's chin trembled. "Like she always did. Anyway, it was my choice to become her because I didn't think you'd want me. Please don't think badly of her. She cared for you and was excited to travel west to be your bride." She fell silent but refused to drop her gaze. If he wouldn't forgive her, he'd have to do it to her face.

His eyes narrowed, and his nostrils flared. "Fine. I forgive you." His words dripped with venom. "Happy?"

She rocked back on her heels. "I-It's not about me being happy. Yvonne said now that I'm forgiven, I need to ask forgiveness from those I've harmed."

"What?"

"I..uh...I accepted Jesus as my Savior. I'm a believer now."

"When? How?" He rubbed his forehead.

"Five days ago. Yvonne found me after...well, you know...and she took me home. We talked a lot, and I read her Bible. I'm going to be staying with them for the near future, so I can study with her and learn." Rayne shrugged. "I should leave town, but they insisted that I remain with them. They've been so gracious and have promised to stand up with me at church tomorrow when I ask forgiveness from the congregation. I'm telling you this so you can stay home if you want." Perspiration pooled under her arms. "Then I'll...uh...attend the other church in town so you won't have to see me."

His frozen veneer finally seemed to crack, one corner of his mouth tilted up. "I'm pleased you've come to know the Lord."

"Thank you—"

"But that doesn't change anything between us."

"I know." Her voice caught. "I don't expect it to. I've wounded you too deeply, but I hope after a time you will heal and can find happiness with someone else. Oh, and I've written a letter to Mrs. Crenshaw apologizing to her as well, so you may be hearing from her."

"All right." Uncertainty flitted across his face. "You don't need to attend the other church. If our folks are willing to let you stay, who am I to demand that you go elsewhere?"

"You're—"

"It was a rhetorical question. Now, have you said all you've come to say?"

"Yes. Thank you for seeing me. I wish you the best, Flynn." She turned on her heel, and tears spilled down her cheeks. She slipped out the door before she lost control completely. Rushing to the wagon, she hefted herself onto the seat and bowed her head. *Help me, Lord. Without Your strength, I'm never going to get over him.*

Chapter Twenty-Two

Flynn stopped pacing long enough to stare out the living room window. Dark, swollen clouds scudded across the overcast skies. By the look of it, rain wasn't far behind. The streets were empty, Rocky Mountain Springs' citizens either smart enough to avoid the weather or already ensconced at church. Where he should be.

Fortunately, Rayne had warned him of her intention to bare her soul to the congregation today, so he could remain at home to avoid the mortification of knowing that everyone realized he'd been taken for a fool. Of course, they'd still know tomorrow, but he'd experience their pity one by one as they came into the store rather than as a group. Their faces lined with compassion, they'd bestow platitudes aimed at making him feel less stupid. Claiming any one of them could have been hoodwinked by her actions. And had been.

He worked side by side with her for days. Hours of thinking he knew who she was yet not having a clue. He groaned. What an idiot. Proof he was unprepared for any sort of relationship, especially marriage.

Thunder cracked, and he jumped. Pressing a hand against his chest, he turned and grabbed the soiled dishes from the table. He dumped them into the sink and winced when the plate cracked in half. He scooped the broken china into the trash, then worked the pump until water poured out of the spigot. He washed and dried his coffee cup and utensils, then put them away.

Pivoting on his heel, he raked his gaze over the rest of the house. Neat as a pin thanks to a frenzied bout of cleaning after he'd come home from work last night. He'd hoped the activity would take his mind off the conversation with Rayne, but thoughts swirled and collided as he cleared clutter, then dusted, swept, and mopped. Sweaty and exhausted, he'd taken a bath and fallen into bed, but sleep had eluded him. He'd fought with the covers most of the night as images and snippets of their exchange marched through his brain.

There was paperwork to be done at the shop. Perhaps wading through orders and invoices would distract him. No, not on a Sunday. It was bad enough he'd not gone to church, but to conduct business went against everything he believed in. He dropped onto the couch and put his head in his hands. *Dear God, I'm at a loss here. Mrs. Crenshaw and I both prayed about my potential bride, yet You allowed us to be taken in by a fraud. How is that part of Your plan? Am I supposed to grow or learn a lesson? Well, I've learned you can't trust people.*

A knock sounded, and his head jerked up. "Who is it?" he growled.

The banging continued.

He huffed out a deep breath, pushed to his feet, and clomped to the door. He yanked on the knob.

"Aren't you in fine fettle." Alonzo grinned at him. "You gonna let me in?"

"What are you doing here?" Flynn frowned. "In *fine fettle*."

Alonzo chuckled and shouldered his way into the house. "Who better to share the burden of wallowing in misery than one's best friend?"

"I'm not wallowing." Flynn winced at the whine that colored his words. "Anyway, I have a right to my feelings. And if you're going to be sarcastic and obviously unsupportive, I suggest you go away."

"You can't get rid of me that easily." Alonzo sniffed the air. "You've still got coffee? I could use a cup."

Flynn gestured to the stove. "Help yourself."

"Wonderful." Whistling, his friend strode to the cabinet, pulled out a mug, and poured the dark brew to the rim. He raised an eyebrow. "Needed the strong stuff today, did you?"

With a shrug, Flynn flopped into one of the chairs at the table.

Alonzo pulled out a chair with the toe of his boot and sat, then grabbed the sugar bowl and dumped several teaspoons into his coffee. He took a sip, and his mouth twisted. "Well, that will put hair on my chest."

He set down the mug. "Look, I understand why you're upset. Rayne pulled a fast one on you, so you've got a bundle of emotions raging inside: anger, hurt, surprise, and who knows what else."

"And you know this because..."

"I'm more than just a cattle wrangler." Alonzo's mouth crooked in a wry smile. "And being married to Yvonne has taught me more than you can imagine."

"Makes you talk about your feelings, does she?" Flynn snorted a laugh. "Bet that's interesting."

"Look, I love you like a brother, Flynn, but sometimes that means saying the hard stuff." He ran his finger around the rim of the mug. "And you're making this situation all about you, rather than Rayne. You can't do that."

"And why not?" Flynn banged his fist on the table, and the coffee sloshed. "She wronged me."

"Yes, she did, but she's repented her actions." Alonzo squeezed Flynn's hand. "And she's joined the family of God. Another lost soul has entered the kingdom. A cause for rejoicing, wouldn't you say?"

Flynn's stomach lurched, and his throat thickened. He sent his friend a grudging nod. "Yes, but..."

"But nothing. Nursing a wound and clinging to an unforgiving attitude is also a sin. And the last time I checked, God doesn't rank our wrongdoings, so what you're doing is just as bad as what she put you through."

"I told her last night I forgave her."

"Really? Because staying home from church and not supporting her is a funny way of showing it.

"Ouch."

"I'm not trying to be mean, Flynn, but as believers we're called to hold each other accountable." Alonzo tilted his chair. "Look, we've all had our moments of being less than honorable, but I think there's more going on than you'll admit. Perhaps this is about your family. You never talk about them, so something happened to make you flee your homeland. Or could it be that you love Rayne, and you don't know how to reconcile your affections with your anger?"

"Jessica was supposed to be my wife. I'd be disloyal to her if I forget about her and marry her sister." Flynn's chest tightened. "Even if she is the one who told Rayne to come."

Alonzo's eyes widened. "What?"

Flynn lifted a shoulder in a halfhearted shrug. "When she realized she was dying, she told Rayne to take her place."

"You are a mess, aren't you?" Alonzo grinned, righted the chair, then rose. "If your original intended sent her sister, I'm pretty sure you're not being disloyal. Now, it's time for you to grab your hat, and go tell that woman how you feel about her. Before some other guy snatches her out from under your nose."

Stomach fluttering as if a swarm of hummingbirds had taken flight, Flynn jumped up. "You're right, and I've been too blind to see it." He grabbed Alonzo in a bear hug. "Thank you, friend, for setting me straight." He raced to the door, grabbed his Stetson, and left the house, Alonzo on his heels. His pulse skittered. Would she see clear to forgive him?

Breathless, he arrived at the church. He straightened his spine and whipped off his hat. He opened the door and stepped inside. His gaze went to the front where Rayne stood next to Pastor Taggart.

Her face was wet with tears. "Thank you for listening to me. I hope you find it in your hearts to forgive me."

The congregation began to talk among themselves, their buzzing voices filling the sanctuary.

She lifted her chin and met Flynn's eyes, her expression one of pain and uncertainty.

His heart pounded as he rushed forward. He arrived at her side and took her hand in his. Tingles shot up his arms, and he sighed. He did love this woman, no matter what she'd done. He lifted his other hand. "Can I have your attention, folks?"

Silence fell.

"Thank you." He glanced at Rayne, whose eyes were riveted on his face. He lowered one eyelid in a slow wink, and she flushed. He stroked the back of her hand with his thumb and turned back to the crowd. "Listen, I know this is a lot to take in. I only heard about it myself last night, and I was full of anger, righteous anger, or so I thought until a friend helped me see the light."

He blew out a loud breath. "What Miss Dalton did was wrong, but we didn't walk in her shoes. Who are we to judge her and refuse to grant forgiveness when she's asked for it? Not to get preachy, but I'm reminded of the story about the woman caught in adultery. Jesus encouraged the folks who had no sin to throw the first stone, but none of them qualified. Don't be like me and the Pharisee. Don't hang on to judgment that isn't yours to give."

Pastor Taggart puffed out his chest. "Thank you, son. I couldn't have said it better myself."

From the back of the room, someone clapped their hands, then a second person joined, then another until the applause swelled. Someone whistled, and several of the men tossed their hats in the air.

Flynn peeked at Rayne. Shock and joy warred for supremacy, and her tear-filled eyes met his. Heart hammering in his chest, he beamed at her. How could he have almost turned her away? He lowered himself to one knee and took both her hands in his, and the ovation ceased, the congregation drawing a collective breath. "Rayne, I love you more than life itself. Would you do me the honor of forgiving this fool of a man and becoming my wife?"

Her eyes widened, and she gasped as she seemed to search his face.

The moment stretched, and his smile faltered. "I'm so—"

"Yes and yes." Rayne's face glowed. "I love you, too."

He leapt to his feet and pulled her into his arms. Cheering and applause filled the sanctuary again as he lowered his head and pressed his lips to hers.

July 1872

Epilogue

A warm breeze fluttered the kitchen curtains as Rayne finished frosting the chocolate layer cake. She stepped back and studied the fragrant confection with a smile, then glanced at the watch pinned to her bodice. Another two hours until Flynn would close the mercantile and come home. Plenty of time to decorate the living room and hang the large paper banner the Sunday school children had made for the birthday party.

Twice at breakfast, she'd nearly given away the surprise. After kissing her goodbye, he whispered in her ear that he knew she was up to something. She'd studied his face and been relieved to see teasing in his eyes. Even after more than a year of marriage, guilt over her deception flared at unexpected times.

Images of their wedding floated into her mind. Flynn had insisted they marry as quickly as possible, so she and Yvonne had pulled together the ceremony in two weeks. The Delaney sisters had worked their magic with a needle and thread, not only finishing the quilt but creating a beautiful white silk gown bedecked with ribbons and bows and featuring lace collar and cuffs. One of the ladies from church had made a floral crown to which a fingertip veil was attached. She'd never worn such a fancy dress in her life.

The only bittersweet moment during the day had been the words Flynn had spoken about holding missing family members in their hearts and memories. Rayne still wondered about God's plans to take her sister to heaven and send her to Wyoming, but she continued to study the Bible with Yvonne, so perhaps one day she'd understand His mysteries.

She shook her head to clear her thoughts. There was work to be done if everything was going to be prepared in time. She'd wasted almost fifteen minutes ruminating over the past. Standing in front of the sink, she made quick work of the soiled baking dishes, then wiped down the counters and table.

Savory aromas wafted from the oven, and she opened the door, then lifted the lid on the cast-iron pot to peek inside at the beef roast surrounded by root vegetables. Her mouth watered, and she put the lid back in place and closed the oven. Next, she raised the towel on the pan of rolls, pleased to see they were rising on schedule. It had taken her months to get the hang of yeast breads, and Flynn had been gracious about eating the various renditions made through trial and error...mostly error.

Her lips quirked. Bread hadn't been her only challenge while learning how to run a household. More than a few meals had been overcooked to say nothing of her attempts at sewing curtains. She'd finally given up and ordered premade drapes through the catalog. Good thing Flynn owned a mercantile.

Rayne wiped down the furniture with a cloth, then swept the house before crying interrupted her work. She rushed to the mahogany cradle sitting by the fireplace. "Mama's coming, Jessica." She picked up the squalling baby and cuddled her close, the child's downy head soft against Rayne's chin. "Did you have a good nap? Daddy will be home soon." With quick motions she changed the infant's diaper, then cleaned her with a damp cloth and dressed her in the frilly cotton outfit Yvonne had given them for the child's first birthday last month. Flynn had been insistent they name the baby after Rayne's sister, and with each passing day, the baby grew to resemble the aunt she would never meet.

Chores completed, Rayne went to the bedroom, washed up, and changed into her Sunday dress. She brushed her hair and wrestled the thick tresses into a chignon, leaving a curl dangling on either side of her face. Flushed from working, she didn't need to pinch her cheeks to give them color. Footsteps sounded on the porch, and she wagged her finger at her reflection. "Don't give away the secret."

She picked up Jessica from the bed and hurried into the living room to greet Flynn. "Happy birthday, sweetheart."

He wrapped his arms around her and the baby. "How are my two favorite girls?"

"We had a good day, and someone had a nap so she won't be cranky when the Lawtons arrive for dessert."

Taking Jessica from Rayne, he nuzzled the child's nose with his own. "She's never cranky."

"For you." Rayne giggled. "She knows just how to get you to do her bidding. Now, wash your hands; dinner is ready."

With a chuckle, he strolled to the cradle and tucked Jessica inside. She flailed her arms and cooed as he bent and kissed her forehead before heading to the sink.

Rayne bustled around the kitchen, setting the food on the table, then spied the stack of six small plates sitting next to the cake. She gulped and tossed a linen over them, hoping he hadn't noticed the extra china.

Dinner passed quickly, and she stifled the desire to check her watch. How much longer before their friends arrived?

Flynn sat back and rubbed his belly. "A delicious birthday meal, Rayne. I couldn't eat another bite."

She grinned. "Not even a slice of cake?"

"I think I can manage dessert."

A knock sounded, and her heart tripped. Her palms moistened. What if Flynn didn't like his gift? She pinned on a smile and rose, collecting their dirty dishes. "Perfect timing. Can you let in the Lawtons?"

He clattered to his feet and went to the door. Alonzo stood on the threshold, Yvonne behind him. "You need to move aside, birthday boy. Your gift is rather large."

The Lawtons separated, revealing a tall man with dark hair graying at the temples. Dressed in a charcoal-colored waistcoat with matching vest, the man wore gray striped slacks and a silk top hat. A petite woman with blonde hair worn in ringlets stood next to the man. Her mint-green dress complemented her porcelain complexion. She rushed forward and embraced Flynn. "Happy birthday, Flynn."

"Mother? Father?" Brow creased, Flynn looked back and forth between his parents. "What are you doing here?"

Rayne hurried to him and wrapped her arm around his waist. "Happy birthday, sweetheart. I hope you like my gift."

Alonzo nudged Flynn aside. "Don't leave us on the porch all night, *old* man. I believe there's cake to be had."

Flynn blinked and seemed to regain his composure. "Of course. Welcome to my home. This is my wife, Rayne, but you apparently already know that."

His mother grasped Rayne's hand. "Yes, but we've only corresponded. You are more beautiful than I imagined. I'm so glad my son has found love."

Rayne's face heated. His mother was obviously just being polite. Compared to the woman's regal attire, she looked like a country mouse.

Jessica gurgled, and Flynn's mother hastened to the cradle. "And this must be our granddaughter. Percy, come see."

The man strode into the house and bent his large frame over the bed. His face lit up, and he looked at Flynn. "She's lovely, Flynn. As is your wife." His smile faltered. "You've made a good life here. We're proud of what you've accomplished. And...uh...we were wrong to get involved where it was none of our business and send Miss St. George. Can you forgive us?"

His jaw dropped, and he seemed to study his father for a long moment. His mother nodded, and Flynn's gaze moved to her face, a tentative smile clinging to her lips.

He glanced down at Rayne. "You brought them here? How—"

"It's a long story, best enjoyed over cake and coffee." She licked her lips. "But you're not angry that I kept their coming a secret? Miss St. George helped me contact them. We've written several letters, and they were anxious to visit and make things right between you. It was their idea to come for your birthday."

Flynn kissed her cheek, then extended his hand toward his father. "And it's the best gift I could ever wish for."

His father bypassed his hand and swept Flynn into a fierce hug.

Rayne's heart swelled as she looked around the room at the smiling faces. Yvonne had been right. God did work out his plans for good.

What did you think of *Rayne's Redemption?*

Thank you so much for purchasing *Rayne's Redemption.* You could have selected any number of books to read, but you chose this book.

I hope it added encouragement and exhortation to your life. If so, it would be nice if you could share this book with your family and friends by posting to Facebook (www.facebook.com) and/or Twitter (www.twitter.com).

If you enjoyed this book and found some benefit in reading it, I'd appreciate it if you could take some time to post a review on Amazon, Goodreads, Kobo, GooglePlay, Apple Books, or other book review site of your choice. Your feedback and support will help me to improve my writing craft for future projects and make this book even better.
Thank you again for your purchase.

Blessings,
Linda Shenton Matchett

Grab the next release in the Westward Home & Hearts Mail-Order Bride Series, *Sookie's Silence*.

After the accident that kills her parents leaves her mute, Susanna Donaldson grasps at the chance to be a mail-order bride. The only catch is that she must also be able to teach school.

Sookie, her nickname since childhood, taught school for many years. Surely in Nebraska, people will welcome any trained teacher--even one who cannot speak. She fits all the requirements that the matchmaker, Milly Crenshaw, outlines for her. A perfect match, surely.

Will her surly groom send her back on the first train east when he realizes that Sookie is silent? Who is the man who shadows her every movement in her new hometown? Suddenly, Sookie's silence stands in her way of both happiness and safety.

http://www.amazon.com/dp/ B08T6N9TJF

Want more *Westward Home & Hearts* Mail-order Bride romance by Linda Shenton Matchett? Read on for the first chapter of *Dinah's Dilemma*.

May 1870
Lincoln, Nebraska

Chapter One

Nathan Childs raced across the field toward his daughter as she toddled with determination toward the fire. How had he managed to let Florence get so far from his side? The three-year-old was fearless, and he knew better than to give her too much freedom. He'd already prevented her from crawling under the fence into the horse pen and trying to climb one of the massive sugar maples that sheltered the food tables at the town's Memorial Day celebration.

Perspiration trickled down his spine, and his shirt clung to his back as the midday sun beat down on his head and glared into his eyes. The morning had dawned unseasonably warm, and the temperatures continued to rise. Summers in Nebraska were known as scorchers, but May was early to be fighting heat and humidity.

"Florence," he shouted as he ran to gain the child's attention, but his voice was swallowed up in the myriad conversations, music, and laughter of Lincoln's citizens. Nebraska's capital had exploded in population over the last eighteen months, and Burlington and Missouri River Railroad's first train was due at the end of June. Sure to bring even more people. Not what he'd envisioned when he moved West after Georgianna's death.

Finally, close enough to grab her, he scooped Florence into his arms and pressed her close to his chest, her small body warm and soft. "What were you thinking, baby girl? Fire is bad. You need to be more careful and stay near me."

"No!" She arched her back and flailed her legs. "Fire is pretty, Daddy." Her face reddened, and she sobbed as if she'd lost her best friend. Tears dampened her cheeks, her blue eyes swimming.

His heart dropped. He hated when she cried. Her sobs made him feel as helpless as a newborn calf. He never knew what to do when she got like this. He hugged her closer and rubbed circles on her back in an effort to calm her.

"Sounds like someone's tired."

Nathan turned and nodded.

His best friend and the town sheriff, Alfred Denard, approached, a wide grin creasing his face below his black Stetson hat. "How about if you take a break and let Livvy watch her for a while. Looks like you both could use a change of scenery."

"Is it that obvious?"

Alfred chuckled as they headed for the cluster of women seated under the trees. "Sometimes I think you'd rather face the Mes Gang or Farrington Brothers than a crying little girl."

Nathan shrugged. "At least when I was chasing outlaws as a Pinkerton, I'd been trained and knew what to expect. Raising Florence is another whole ball of wax. Every day is different, so something I learned yesterday, doesn't necessarily work today." He blew out a deep breath as Florence quieted and tucked her thumb into her mouth. "I love her with my whole being, but maybe I should have let Georgianna's parents take her. I'm failing miserably."

"Do you think living with her grandparents is what's best for her?"

Nearing the blanket where Alfred's wife, Olivia, sat, Nathan paused and grimaced. "I don't know anymore. The thought of having to decide paralyzes me."

Livvy rose and held out her arms, her blonde hair swept into a tight bun at the base of her neck. She smiled, and her face glowed. "Are you going to let me spend time with your sweet little girl, Nathan? I've been aching to hold that child all day."

Florence chortled and reached for the buxom young woman. Nathan transferred his daughter into her waiting embrace, and his arms felt bereft. He shoved his hands into his pockets.

"Can I keep her through dinner, Nathan?" Livvy poked Florence's belly then rubbed noses with the giggling youngster. "We'll have lots of fun together, won't we?"

"You sure that's not too much time, Livvy?"

She shook her head. "Not enough, if you ask me." She jerked her head toward the corrals. "You boys head over to the pens and enjoy yourselves. The roping competitions should be starting soon."

Alfred ran his finger along her jaw then kissed her cheek, a starry-eyed look on his face. Married for three years, he still mooned over his wife, like a besotted schoolboy. Livvy had come from Atlanta as his friend's mail-order bride. Claiming love at first sight, they'd married immediately. "You holler if you need help, honey."

"I'll be fine." She winked at her husband. "Now, scoot."

Nathan pressed his lips together as his heart tugged. It had been too long since anyone looked at him like Livvy gazed at Alfred, but he had enough going on without saddling himself with a wife. He turned toward the festivities.

He couldn't ask for better friends than Alfred and Livvy. Two days after he'd arrived fifteen months ago, they'd shown up at his claim with food and friendship. Between the two of them, they'd arranged for some of the locals to transport his supplies from Omaha then pulled together a cadre of men to help build the house and barn. Livvy kept him fed when he didn't feel like eating in those early days of mourning after Georgianna's death. He'd figured moving to a new location would lessen the hollow feeling in his heart since she'd never lived in Nebraska, but his grief had followed him.

A city girl born and bred, she would have hated life on the plains, but he still missed her presence. Especially in the small things. Rustling up a stack of pancakes or sitting on the front porch watching the sun dip behind the trees, talking about everything and nothing.

The first year in Lincoln had been difficult, but rewarding. The crop had been decent, and he'd put aside some money for the future. Maybe to purchase the adjoining plot. Too soon to do so, but the idea was tempting. This year's wheat had done well and would be ready to harvest in another couple of months.

A stiff gust kicked up dust from the animal enclosures and swirled above the beasts. The acrid smell of manure clung to the breeze as it lifted his hat. Would he ever get used to the constant wind?

"All right, gents, time to see who's the best roper in the Lincoln." Barnard Johnson, a cattle rancher who owned the largest spread outside of town, stood in the center of one of the corrals, thumbs tucked in the waistband of his denim pants. A pair of ivory-handled pistols, Colts, if Nathan wasn't mistaken, hung from an ornate holster around his substantial belly. His boots gleamed.

Alfred jabbed Nathan with a sharp elbow. "You should take a turn. Show up the rest of the boys."

"No, thanks. I want to make friends not enemies."

"This is just a friendly competition."

"I'll pass, but you should take a turn. Confirm why you're the best sheriff in Nebraska."

"Because I can lasso the outlaws?" Alfred's chuckle rumbled in his chest. "Think I'll pass, too."

"Hey, Nathan. Aren't you going to show off those muscles of yours?"

Nathan cringed at the sound of Katrina Wainwright's strident voice that could send dogs and bats running for cover. She'd made her intentions clear at Christmas that he was the man for her despite his protestations to the contrary. Not one to be put off easily, she turned up at his side every chance she got. He squared his shoulders and pivoted on his heel.

Dipping his head in greeting, he forced a smile. "Good afternoon, Miss Wainwright. Are you enjoying today's event?"

Her giggle ended with a snort as she slapped his arm. "Katrina. How many times do I have to remind you to call me by my given name?"

"It wouldn't be proper, Miss Wainwright."

"We're not exactly in a Boston drawing room."

"True—"

"Hey, Katrina, watch this!" From inside the corral, one of Mr. Johnson's cowhands waved his hands over his head.

She turned, and Nathan took the opportunity to escape. Alfred followed close behind him. They strode to the six-foot tables piled with platters of food, grabbed a couple of plates, and chose several delicious-looking items. Nathan frowned. "That was a close one, but I feel bad for sneaking away."

"Don't. You've made it clear you're not interested. And after the incident with Florence when she took the child from the church nursery without your permission, she ought to know you'll never trust her." Alfred held an oatmeal cookie up to his nose and took a deep breath. "I do love my wife's baking." He took a bite and grinned. Shoving the rest of the treat into his mouth, he clapped Nathan on the back as he finished chewing. "I know how you can get rid of her."

Nathan narrowed his eyes. "I'm afraid to ask."

"Don't be. I have the perfect solution. You need a substitute girlfriend, and I know where you can get one."

"No. Before you say anything else, the answer is no. I'm not going to apply for a mail-order bride." Tears pricked the backs of his eyes. "You and Livvy are very happy, but I'm not in the market for a wife, and I don't think I'll ever be." He swallowed against the lump that had formed in his throat.

"I understand your grief. Don't forget I lost my first wife six years ago. But you can find love again. Unfortunately, the ratio of women to men out here isn't good, and your choices in Lincoln are limited." He wiggled his eyebrows. "Unless, you'd like to reconsider Miss Wainwright."

"Absolutely not." Nathan shuddered. "Despite her outward beauty, she's deceitful, and I could never love a woman like that. Florence and I are doing just fine with the two of us."

"Are you so sure about that? Your little girl needs a mother. You're not being fair to Florence. Please think about contacting Milly Crenshaw at the Westward Home and Hearts Matrimonial Agency." He squeezed Nathan's shoulder. "Now, as much as I enjoy time with you, I'm going to sit with my beautiful wife."

Nathan watched him leave, a jaunty air in his step as he threaded his way through the crowd to Livvy. She beamed as he approached then blushed after he bent and whispered something in her ear.

Was Alfred right? Could he find a woman he would love as he had Georgianna? He surveyed the townspeople, his gaze stopping to rest on Katrina. Full figured with a peaches-and-cream complexion, she had ebony-colored hair and deep-brown eyes. A gorgeous woman evidenced by the number of young men crowding around her like a flock of chicks.

But he couldn't get past her subterfuge. Plain and simple, she'd lied then claimed the whole thing was a misunderstanding. Should he try to find an honest woman who would love Florence as her own? Did this Milly Crenshaw have the answer? Surely, anyone she sent couldn't be any worse than Katrina.

Acknowledgments

Although writing a book is a solitary task, it is not a solitary journey. There have been many who have helped and encouraged me along the way.

My parents, Richard and Jean Shenton, who presented me with my first writing tablet and encouraged me to capture my imagination with words. Thanks, Mom and Dad!

Scribes212 – my ACFW online critique group: Valerie Goree, Marcia Lahti, and the late Loretta Boyett (passed on to Glory, but never forgotten). Without your input, my writing would not be nearly as effective.

Eva Marie Everson – my mentor/instructor with Christian Writers' Guild. You took a timid, untrained student and turned her into a writer. Many thanks!

SincNE, and the folks who coordinate the Crimebake Writing Conference. I have attended many writing conferences, but without a doubt, Crimebake is one of the best. The workshops, seminars, panels, critiques, and every tiny aspect are well-executed, professional, and educational.

Special thanks to Hank Phillippi Ryan, Halle Ephron, and Roberta Isleib for your encouragement and spot-on critiques of my work.

Thanks to my Book Brigade who provide information, encouragement, and support.

Paula Proofreader (https://paulaproofreader.wixsite.com/home): I'm so glad I found you! My work is cleaner because of your eagle eye. Any mistakes are completely mine.

A heartfelt thank you to my brothers, Jack Shenton and Douglas Shenton, and my sister, Susan Shenton Greger for being enthusiastic cheerleaders during my writing journey. Your support means more than you'll know.

My husband, Wes, deserves special kudos for understanding my need to write. Thank you for creating my writing room – it's perfect, and I'm thankful for it every day. Thank you for your willingness to accept a house that's a bit cluttered, laundry that's not always done, and meals on the go. I love you.

And finally, to God be the glory. I thank Him for giving me the gift of writing and the inspiration to tell stories that shine the light on His goodness and mercy.

Other Titles
Romance

Love's Harvest, Wartime Brides, Book 1

Love's Rescue, Wartime Brides, Book 2

Love's Belief, Wartime Brides, Book 3

Love's Allegiance, Wartime Brides, Book 4

Love Found in Sherwood Forest

A Love Not Forgotten

On the Rails

A Doctor in the House

Spies & Sweethearts, Sisters in Service, Book 1

The Mechanic & the MD, Sisters in Service, Book 2

The Widow & the War Correspondent, Sisters in Service, Book 3

Love at First Flight

Multi-author Series

A Bride for Seamus (Proxy Brides, 48)

Dinah's Dilemma (Westward Home and Hearts Mail-Order Brides, 10)

Legacy of Love (Keepers of the Light, 10)

Vanessa's Replacement Valentine, Brides of Pelican Rapids, 13)

Mystery

Under Fire, Ruth Brown Mystery Series, Book 1

Under Ground, Ruth Brown Mystery Series, Book 2

Under Cover, Ruth Brown Mystery Series, Book 3

Murder of Convenience, Women of Courage, Book 1

Murder at Madison Square Garden, Women of Courage, Book 2

Non-Fiction

WWII Word Find, Volume 1

Biography

Linda Shenton Matchett writes about ordinary people who did extraordinary things in days gone by. She is a volunteer docent and archivist at the Wright Museum of WWII and a trustee for her local public library. Born in Baltimore, Maryland, a stone's throw from Fort McHenry, she has lived in historical places most of her life. Now located in central New Hampshire, Linda's favorite activities include exploring historical sites and immersing herself in the imaginary worlds created by other authors.

Website/blog: http://www.LindaShentonMatchett.com
Newsletter signup (receive a free short story):
https://mailchi.mp/74bb7b34c9c2/lindashentonmatchettnewsletter
Facebook: http://www.facebook.com/LindaShentonMatchettAuthor
Pinterest: http://www.pinterest.com/lindasmatchett
Amazon: https://www.amazon.com/Linda-Shenton-Matchett/e/B01DNB54S0
Goodreads: http://www.goodreads.com/author_linda_matchett
Bookbub: http://www.bookbub.com/authors/linda-shenton-matchett